# THE MILL GIRL

SYBIL COOK

# CHAPTER 1

arah

SARAH DOBBS KEPT her head down and her mouth shut. This wasn't particularly difficult in St. Michael's Workhouse, where both habits were beaten into children from the moment they arrived. Having spent 10 years grim establishment, Sarah had mastered the art of being invisible.

But not today.

"What'd you call this, girl? Stitching or chicken scratch?" Matron Grimsby held up little Lily's sewing work, shaking it in the frightened child's face. "I've seen blind beggars do better!"

Lily's bottom lip wobbled dangerously. At seven years old, she was the youngest in the sewing room, and her tiny fingers still struggled with the needle.

Sarah fought the urge to roll her eyes. Matron Grimsby stood with her hands planted on her substantial hips, waiting for tears. She always waited for tears.

"I'm sorry, Matron," Lily whispered.

"Sorry won't mend the shirts, will it? Sorry won't earn your keep!" Matron raised her to strike, and Sarah's decision was made before she even knew she'd made it.

"I'll fix it," Sarah said, standing up from her workbench.

Twenty pairs of eyes snapped toward her in horror. Speaking unbidden was against the rules. Volunteering for extra work? Unheard of.

Matron Grimsby turned slowly, her small eyes narrowing to mean little points. "What was that, Dobbs?"

"I said I'll fix it," Sarah repeated. "I've finished my batch already. I can redo Lily's seams before supper."

"Oh? The great Sarah Dobbs will save the day?" Matron's smile was worse than her frown. "How wonderfully charitable. And when exactly did you become mistress of this workhouse?"

Sarah bit her tongue. Hard. "I didn't mean…"

"You didn't mean to overstep? To question my authority?" Matron strode over, and leaned down until her face was inches from Sarah's. Her breath smelled of stale tea and spite. "I've had my eye on you, Dobbs and you're 5oo smart for your own good. Too proud by half."

Sarah stood her ground but lowered her gaze as expected. "No, Matron."

"Mark my words, girl." Matron's voice dropped to a venomous whisper. "The world loves nothing more than breaking the spirit of proud girls like you. It's coming for you, and I'll enjoy watching when it does." She straightened up. "Take the work. Both of you will miss supper."

Sarah nodded. No beating, at least.

The sewing room door creaked open, and Mr. Simmons, the workhouse master, poked his balding head inside. "Matron Grimsby, a word?"

Matron Grimsby huffed but followed him out, closing the door with force.

Lily scurried over to Sarah's bench, her eyes wide and teary. "I'm sorry, Sarah. You shouldn't have…"

"Shh." Sarah smiled, running a hand over Lily's tangled hair. "It's alright. Let me see this terrible chicken scratch."

Lily giggled then handed over the poorly hemmed shirt.

"It's not so bad," Sarah lied, examining the crooked stitches. "You're getting better. Here, watch how I hold the needle."

The girls worked in blessed silence for ten minutes before the door banged open again and Matron Grimsby strode in, looking insufferably pleased.

"Well, girls," she said, rubbing her hands together. "This is a happy day indeed." Her tone suggested it was anything but. "Stoops, Dobbs, Miller, Rhodes, and Thompson, come front and center!"

Sarah exchanged a quick glance with Amanda, her closest friend in this wretched place. Amanda's eyebrows drew together in concern.

The five girls stood before Matron, who circled them like a cat toying with mice.

"Such luck! Such opportunity!" Matron declared. "Bailey's Cotton Mill needs new workers, and Mr. Simmons has kindly offered your services."

Sarah's stomach dropped. The mill. Everyone knew what happened to children in the mills.

"You'll depart immediately. Pack your things." Matron's grin was pure shark.

The mill was brutal, but it was... outside. Away from St. Michael's and away from Matron Grimsby.

As the other girls hurried out, Matron caught Sarah's arm in a bony vise. "A special word for you, Dobbs," she hissed. "Cause any trouble at Bailey's, and you won't be coming back here. Not ever."

Sarah tried to pull away, but Matron held fast.

"The mills don't tolerate troublemakers. Get yourself dismissed, and there's only one place that takes ruined girls." She smiled coldly. "Madame Abbess is always looking for fresh faces at her bawdy house. Remember that when your pride gets the better of you."

Sarah wrenched her arm free, ignoring the sting of fingernail marks on her skin. "Yes, Matron," she said.

Anywhere, she thought fiercely. Anywhere but here.

THE CART JOLTED over yet another pothole, sending Sarah crashing against Amanda's shoulder.

"Sorry," she muttered, straightening herself.

Amanda gave her a weak smile. "We're nearly there."

The five girls huddled together on hard wooden benches, their few belongings tied in small bundles at their feet. Four boys from another workhouse sat across from them, looking just as grim.

Outside the cart's small window, Lancashire's industrial landscape rolled by with gray buildings belching darker gray smoke into the already gray sky. It might have been depressing if Sarah hadn't spent her entire life staring at St. Michael's grimy walls.

"Do you know what it's like?" Sarah whispered to Amanda. "The mill, I mean."

Amanda's face tightened. "My cousin worked at one before she died. She said the noise never stops and you breathe cotton more than air."

"Sounds wonderful," Sarah said dryly.

Amanda snorted, then quickly covered her mouth. Sarah grinned.

The cart lurched to a stop, sending them all scrambling to stay on the benches.

"End of the line, workhouse rats!" the driver called cheerfully. "Welcome to your new prison!"

Sarah climbed down first, then helped the others. Before them stood Bailey's Cotton Mill, a monstrous brick building with tall chimneys spewing black smoke that seemed to swallow the sky.

"Not exactly promising, is it?" Sarah murmured to Amanda.

"Better than Grimsby's lovely face every morning," Amanda replied.

The workhouse master emerged from the cart's front seat, straightening his waistcoat importantly. "This way, children. Be on your best behavior now."

They were led through large iron gates into a courtyard, where two figures awaited them. A thin, sour-faced man with yellowed teeth stood beside a tight-lipped woman in a severe black dress.

"The new batch, Mr. Thorne," said the workhouse master, handing over a sheaf of papers.

Mr. Thorne's eyes crawled over them like insects, assessing their worth pound by pound.

"Scrawny," he pronounced finally. "But they'll do."

The woman stepped forward. "I am Mrs. Pickering. I manage the female dormitories." Her voice could have frozen water. "You will address me as Ma'am or Mrs. Pickering. Nothing else."

Sarah fought the urge to curtsy mockingly. Another tyrant in different clothes.

"Boys, you're for the carding room," Mr. Thorne barked. "Girls..." His eyes narrowed as he examined each of them. "You three to the weaving shed. Stoops and Dobbs to spinning."

"Get someone to show them their stations," he told Mrs. Pickering. "I want them working tomorrow at dawn." With that, he turned on his heel and stalked away.

Mrs. Pickering's thin lips pressed into an even thinner line. "Briggs! Parker!" she called out.

A boy and girl emerged from a nearby doorway. The boy was tall and wiry with unruly reddish-brown hair and a face full of mischief. The girl was as tall as the boy with blonde, slightly curly hair tucked into a scarf.

"Show the new ones their dormitories and explain the rules," Mrs. Pickering instructed. "Briggs, you take the boys. Parker, the girls."

"Yes, Ma'am," they chorused

Mrs. Pickering fixed Sarah with a penetrating stare. "You. Dobbs, isn't it? You look like trouble."

Sarah blinked innocently. "Me, Ma'am? Never."

Annie quickly stepped forward. "I'll keep an eye on her, Ma'am."

"See that you do." Mrs. Pickering sniffed before marching away.

The boy - Briggs - winked at them before shepherding the new boys toward a separate building. Sarah noticed Annie blush slightly.

"This way," Annie said, leading them into a brick building adjacent to the mill. "I'm Anniette Parker, so you can call me Annie like everyone does."

"I'm Sarah Dobbs" Sarah said unnecessarily, since Annie had clearly heard her name already.

"'Tis nice to meet you," Annie replied with a small smile.

They climbed a narrow staircase to the top floor. "This is the girls' dormitory," Annie explained, pushing open a door to reveal a long room filled with narrow beds. "You'll sleep two to a bed, so get used to being cozy."

The other new girls were shown to their assigned beds, and Sarah bid Amanda goodbye. Then Annie led Sarah to the very end of the room, near a small window.

"You'll bunk with me," she said, gesturing to a straw mattress that looked only marginally better than the ones at St. Michael's. "Mrs. Pickering runs tight quarters. No talking after lights out. No food in the dormitory. Bed linens changed once a month, whether they need it or not." She lowered her voice. "And no personal items on display."

Sarah nodded as she unpacked her pitiful bundle

of a spare dress, undergarments, a thin nightgown, and a small wooden comb.

Annie watched her, then said, "It's not so bad once you get used to it. The work is hard, but at least they feed you regular." She hesitated. "And... well, you're not locked in at night. Sometimes we slip out to the meadow when the weather's nice."

Sarah looked up in surprise. "You can go outside? Whenever you want?"

"Not exactly. There's curfew. But old Mrs. Pickering sleeps like the dead once she's had her nightcap." Annie grinned. "Tommy - that's Briggs - knows all the best ways in and out."

Sarah's fingers went to her neck, where she kept her most prized possession hidden under her dress. It was a small silver locket containing a scrap of paper with her parents' names. It was her only connection to the mother and father she barely remembered.

Annie's eyes widened. "You'd best hide that better," she whispered urgently. "Mrs. Pickering hates jewelry. Says it gives girls ideas about seducing men."

Sarah quickly tucked the locket deeper into her bodice. "It's all I have of my parents," she admitted.

Annie's face softened. "I understand. But be careful. Thorne searches new girls sometimes, looking for valuables."

Sarah's hand instinctively covered the spot where her locket lay hidden. "I'll be careful."

"Get some sleep," Annie helped Sarah make up the bed. "Dawn comes early here, and the overseers don't tolerate tardiness."

Later that night, after the lamps were extinguished and the other girls' breathing had settled, Sarah carefully extracted her locket and held it in her palm. The silver caught the faint moonlight from the window.

She opened it and touched the small scrap of yellowed paper that had two names written in faded ink, James and Mary Dobbs. Her mother had taught her to read those names and more before the fever took both her parents, leaving seven-year-old Sarah to the mercy of St. Michael's.

Sarah closed her eyes, clutching the locket to her chest, and did what she always did before sleep. She imagined her mother's voice singing her to sleep, her father's laugh as he told stories by candlelight. In her mind, their faces were blurry because time had stolen their features, but the feeling of being loved remained clear as day.

Tomorrow she would start her work at the mill

with its noise and dust and endless work. But tonight, in the darkness of her new dormitory, Sarah Dobbs held tight to the only thing that truly belonged to her, the memory of once being someone's daughter.

## CHAPTER 2

aniel

THE CARRIAGE WHEELS clattered over cobblestone streets as Daniel Bailey watched Lancashire grow from a smudge on the horizon to the sprawling industrial town he'd left behind three years ago. The familiar soot-stained buildings came into view, but something was different.

"The mill has grown," Daniel observed, leaning forward to get a better look at Bailey's Cotton Mill. What had once been an impressive but modest structure now dominated the landscape, new wings extending in three directions and additional chimneys pumping black smoke into the already gray sky.

"Your father's been busy," Arthur Evans remarked from his seat across from Daniel. Though technically Daniel's valet, Arthur had been his companion since childhood, the two boys growing up side by side despite their vastly different stations.

Reginald Farnsworth, Daniel's university friend who'd accompanied him for the journey, nudged Daniel with his boot. "Good Lord, look at that woman!" He pointed through the window at a stout female figure in a shabby dress. "She waddles like my aunt's prized goose!"

Daniel didn't laugh. "That 'goose' has probably been standing for twelve hours straight at a loom."

"Oh come now, Bailey. Don't be so dreadfully serious," Reginald huffed, straightening his perfectly tailored jacket. "Cambridge has turned you into a proper bore."

"Perhaps Cambridge has simply opened my eyes," Daniel replied, turning his attention back to the window.

The carriage slowed as they approached the mill. Workers were changing shifts, and a stream of gaunt figures poured from the main doors. Daniel caught glimpses of their hollow cheeks, stooped shoulders, and eyes too old for young faces. Many paused to watch the grand Bailey carriage pass, their expressions one of resentment and resignation.

"They look thinner than I remember," Daniel murmured.

Arthur cleared his throat. "Your father cut the meal allowance last year. He said it was making workers sluggish."

Daniel's jaw tightened. "Sluggish? After fourteen-hour shifts?"

"Sixteen now, sir. When orders are heavy."

The carriage turned off the main road, leaving the mill behind and rolling through ornate gates that marked Bailey property. The difference was immediately noticeable - immaculate gardens replaced industrial grime. The air was suddenly clearer, and the world noticeably quieter.

"Home sweet home," Reginald said, gesturing at the stately manor house that appeared around the bend. "You Baileys certainly know how to live."

Daniel nodded absently, watching a pair of gardeners prune a perfectly shaped hedge. Their faces were full and healthy compared to the mill workers they'd just passed. The irony wasn't lost on him.

The carriage came to a stop at the front entrance,

where a line of servants stood ready to welcome the young master home. At their center stood Elizabeth Bailey, Daniel's mother, her hands clasped tightly before her as if preventing herself from rushing forward prematurely.

"Your mother looks well," Arthur noted as the footman opened the carriage door.

Daniel stepped down, wondering if they were looking at the same woman. His mother's face was thinner than he remembered, and new lines were etched around her eyes and mouth. Her smile, though genuine, seemed to require effort.

"Daniel," she called, propriety forgotten as she hurried down the steps and embraced him. "My darling boy."

"Mother," Daniel returned the embrace, alarmed at how fragile she felt in his arms. "Are you well? You seem…"

"Nonsense," she cut him off. "I'm perfectly fine. Just eager to have you home where you belong."

Daniel pulled back to study her face, but she quickly turned her attention to Reginald, who had followed Daniel from the carriage.

"Mr. Farnsworth, how lovely to see you again. I trust your journey was pleasant?"

"Splendid, Mrs. Bailey," Reginald replied with a

bow. "Though your son spent most of it with his nose buried in books. Terribly antisocial."

Elizabeth laughed politely. "That's our Daniel..."

She turned and gestured toward the house. "Come inside, both of you. I've had the Cook prepare all your favorites, Daniel. And Mr. Farnsworth, I've put you in the blue guest room. I hope that suits."

"Perfectly, ma'am," Reginald said, already heading up the steps, where the butler relieved him of his hat and gloves.

Daniel lingered, taking his mother's arm. "Mother, truly. Are you unwell?"

"I'm fine, Daniel," she insisted, patting his hand. "Just a bit tired. Running this household isn't getting any easier with age."

Daniel wasn't convinced. "And Father? How is he?"

"Busy. Always busy. The mill consumes him more each year." She sighed but quickly brightened up. "But he's terribly excited to see you. He's arranged to be home early for dinner."

They climbed the steps together, Daniel conscious of how she leaned on him more than she once had.

"Go on up and dress for dinner," Elizabeth

instructed as they entered the grand foyer. "Arthur has already taken your things to your room."

Daniel glanced up the sweeping staircase to see Arthur directing footmen carrying his trunks. "Very well, Mother. But we'll speak later?"

"Of course, dear." She smiled, but her eyes darted away from his. "Later."

Daniel stood by his bedroom window, freshly dressed for dinner in a tailored black suit that felt stiff and formal after his casual university attire. From here, he could see the mill in the distance, still operating despite the late hour, its windows lit with gas lamps that turned it into a glowing monster against the darkening sky.

A soft knock at the door preceded Arthur's entrance.

"Ready, sir?"

Daniel turned from the window. "As I'll ever be." He gestured out at the mill. "They're still working."

"The night shift started an hour ago," Arthur explained, brushing an invisible speck from Daniel's shoulder. "Your father extended operations after installing the gas lighting."

"More profit, more misery," Daniel muttered.

Arthur's face remained carefully neutral. "I couldn't say, sir."

"But you could, Arthur. You always see everything."

"Perhaps. But it's not my place to comment on your father's business practices." Arthur handed Daniel his pocket watch. "Master Farnsworth is already downstairs, entertaining your mother with tales of your Cambridge exploits."

Daniel groaned. "God knows what he's telling her."

"Nothing too damaging, I'm sure." Arthur's lips twitched slightly. "Though he did mention something about a stolen pig and the Dean's carriage?"

"That was entirely Farnsworth's doing," Daniel protested. "I was merely an innocent bystander."

"Of course, sir," Arthur replied with the faintest hint of disbelief.

They shared a brief smile before Daniel sobered. "Arthur, be honest. How bad has it gotten? At the mill, I mean."

Arthur hesitated. "There have been... incidents... accidents, and your father pushes for more production every quarter."

"And the workers?"

"They bear it. What choice do they have?"

Daniel nodded grimly. "What choice indeed."

The dinner gong sounded from below, saving Arthur from further uncomfortable questions.

"You're expected, sir," he said with obvious relief.

Daniel straightened his jacket. "Into battle, then."

The Bailey dining room gleamed with polished silver and crystal. A massive chandelier cast warm light over the long mahogany table, set for four with the family's finest china. Elizabeth Bailey sat at one end, looking small against the high-backed chair, while Reginald Farnsworth entertained her with animated stories.

Daniel entered silently, pausing in the doorway to observe the scene. His mother laughed at something Reginald said, but the sound was hollow, her eyes constantly drifting toward the empty chair at the head of the table.

"Ah, Daniel," Reginald called, spotting him. "I was just telling your mother about Professor Whitcombe's spectacular explosion in the chemistry laboratory."

"I hope you're making it clear that I was nowhere near the experiment at the time," Daniel said, moving to kiss his mother's cheek before taking his seat.

"Where would be the fun in that?" Reginald grinned.

The door burst open, and Edward Bailey strode in, still wearing his mill owner's suit, a thick gold watch chain draped across his substantial waistcoat. At fifty-five, he remained an imposing figure - tall, broad-shouldered, with dark hair now streaked with silver.

"Daniel!" he boomed, crossing the room in swift strides. "My boy! Stand up, let me look at you!"

Daniel rose and found himself enveloped in a bone-crushing embrace that smelled of tobacco and expensive cologne.

"Father," he managed, extracting himself from the hug. "You look well."

"As do you! Cambridge agrees with you, I see." Edward clapped him on the shoulder with enough force to make Daniel stagger slightly. "Though you could use more meat on those bones. Been spending too much time with books and not enough time living, eh?"

"I've been studying, Father. That was rather the point of university."

Edward laughed and turned to Reginald. "Young Farnsworth! Good to see you. How's your father? Still making a fortune in shipping?"

"Indeed, sir," Reginald replied, preening slightly under the attention. "He's just acquired two new vessels for the India route."

"Excellent, excellent." Edward took his seat at the head of the table with a flourish. "We'll have to discuss some cotton exports while you're here. Always good to keep business in the family, so to speak."

Elizabeth rang a small silver bell, and servants appeared as if by magic, bearing trays of steaming food.

"I've had Cook prepare your favorite roast beef, Daniel," Elizabeth said as a footman served him.

"Thank you, Mother." Daniel smiled genuinely for the first time since arriving. "You remembered."

"Of course she did," Edward said, already cutting into his meat. "Your mother remembers everything. It's why she runs this household so splendidly."

The meal proceeded with Edward dominating the conversation, boasting about the mill's expansion and peppering Daniel with questions about his studies. For a while, it almost felt normal, like the family dinners of Daniel's childhood, before he'd understood where their wealth came from.

"So tell me, Daniel," Edward said as the main

course was cleared away. "What did you think of the mill? Impressive expansion, isn't it?"

Daniel set down his wine glass carefully. "It's certainly... larger."

"Larger! My boy, it's the largest mill in the county now," Edward declared proudly. "We've doubled production in three years and profits are up nearly sixty percent."

"And the workers?" Daniel couldn't help asking. "How are they faring with this expansion?"

A slight frown creased Edward's brow. "They're employed, aren't they? Better than starving in the streets or rotting in workhouses."

"But the conditions…"

"Are standard for the industry," Edward cut him off. "Better than most, in fact. We installed those new ventilation shafts last year, at considerable expense."

"After three workers died of lung fever," Daniel said quietly.

An uncomfortable silence fell over the table. Reginald looked between father and son with poorly concealed interest, while Elizabeth stared fixedly at her plate.

Edward's face darkened. "You've been home less than a day, and already you're criticizing how I run my business?"

"I'm simply concerned about..."

"You know nothing about running a mill, boy," Edward snapped. "While you've been debating philosophy with your university friends, I've been keeping this family's empire growing. Those workers should be grateful for the opportunity to earn an honest wage."

"Grateful for sixteen-hour shifts? For children losing fingers in machinery? For..."

"Daniel," Elizabeth interrupted. "Perhaps this isn't the best dinner conversation." She turned to Edward with a strained smile. "Dear, why don't you tell Daniel about the Harringtons' summer ball next month? Catherine specifically asked if Daniel would be attending."

Edward's face shifted from anger so quickly that Daniel almost missed it. "Ah, yes. The Harringtons. Good family, solid business connections. Their daughter Catherine has grown into quite the beauty, I'm told."

Daniel suppressed a groan. "Mother, Father, I've barely been home a day."

"Catherine's quite accomplished," Elizabeth continued as if he hadn't spoken. "She plays the pianoforte beautifully, and her watercolors were featured at the Ladies' Art Exhibition."

"And her father owns the largest textile import business in Lancashire," Edward added with significantly less subtlety. "A match between our families would be... advantageous."

"I'm not interested in an 'advantageous match' right now," Daniel said firmly. "I'd like to learn the business first. Understand how the mill operates."

"Learn the business? Splendid idea!" Edward's mood brightened instantly. "You can start next week. I'll have Henderson show you the ledgers, the inventory systems…"

"I meant the actual operations, Father. The factory floor and the workers' conditions."

Edward's smile faded. "That's hardly necessary. The floor managers handle all that."

"How can I possibly understand our business if I don't understand every aspect of it?"

Elizabeth jumped in before Edward could retort. "I think that's a wonderful idea. Daniel should learn everything, from top to bottom." She gave her husband a meaningful look. "If he's to take over someday, he needs a complete understanding."

Edward grunted, appeased by the mention of succession. "Fine. But don't coddle the workers. They'll take advantage if they sense weakness."

"I'll keep that in mind," Daniel said dryly.

"Now, about Catherine Harrington," Edward continued, returning to his favorite subject. "The girl has had her eye on you for years. A summer engagement would be perfect timing."

"Father, I've only just returned…"

"And you're twenty-two, a university man now. Tis time to think about your future, about the Bailey legacy." Edward leaned forward. "This marriage would secure our position in society for generations. The Harrington connections combined with our manufacturing, We'd be unstoppable."

Daniel looked to his mother for support, but she merely offered a sympathetic smile.

"I need time," Daniel insisted. "To settle in, to learn the business. Marriage is... I'm not ready to consider it yet."

"Nonsense," Edward dismissed with a wave of his hand. "Every man thinks that until he meets the right woman. And Catherine Harrington is exactly right. She's beautiful, well-bred, and connected to all the right families. What more could you want?"

Love, Daniel thought but didn't say.

"At least meet with her," Elizabeth suggested gently. "The Harringtons are hosting a dinner next week. You can meet her and see if you like her."

Daniel sighed, recognizing the futility of further argument. "Very well. A dinner."

"Excellent!" Edward beamed, lifting his wine glass in a toast. "To the future of Bailey Mills - and to advantageous connections!"

As everyone dutifully raised their glasses, Daniel caught his mother's eye. Her smile didn't reach her eyes, and he wondered, not for the first time, if her own "advantageous marriage" had brought her any happiness.

# CHAPTER 3

 arah

SARAH's first thought upon entering the spinning room was that she'd somehow stumbled into hell itself. The noise of hundreds of spinning machines working simultaneously, wood clattering against metal, wheels turning, belts slapping felt like war in her ears. The air hung thick with cotton dust that glittered in the weak sunlight streaming through grimy windows.

"Stay close," Annie shouted next to her ear. "Do exactly as I show you."

Girls and women lined the long rows of spinning

mules, their hands moving in constant motion. Sarah noticed their vacant expressions, and the mechanical way they worked, as if their minds had fled their bodies long ago.

Annie led her to an empty spot at one of the massive machines. "This is a spinning mule," she explained, having to shout despite standing inches away. "You tend this section. Keep the threads from breaking. When they do – and they will – you tie them back together. Fast."

Sarah nodded, watching Annie's hands demonstrate the process.

"Miss Bradshaw oversees this room. We call her The Hawk," Annie continued. "Whatever you do, don't catch her attention."

As if summoned by her name, a tall, sharp-featured woman appeared behind them. Miss Bradshaw had gray eyes that never seemed to blink and thin lips permanently pressed into a disapproving line.

"New girl," she said "Don't coddle her, Parker. Get to your station."

"Yes, Miss Bradshaw." Annie squeezed Sarah's arm before hurrying to her position two machines down.

"Begin," Miss Bradshaw said, her cold eyes boring

into Sarah. "Every broken thread costs Bailey money. Every second you waste costs Bailey money. Remember that."

Sarah turned to the spinning mule, her confidence evaporating as she faced the enormous machine. The threads danced before her eyes, dozens of them, moving too fast to count. How was she supposed to watch them all at once?

Before she could even settle into position, three threads snapped almost simultaneously. Sarah froze, panicked, uncertain which to fix first.

"Move, girl!" Miss Bradshaw barked.

Sarah lunged for the nearest broken thread, trying to remember Annie's demonstration. Her fingers fumbled with the fine cotton, refusing to cooperate.

"Faster!" The single word cracked like a whip.

Sarah managed to tie the first thread, but by then, five more had broken. Her untrained hands were too slow, too clumsy. The machine waited for no one, continuously spinning, creating more broken threads with each passing second.

Miss Bradshaw circled the room, her hawk-like gaze missing nothing. When Sarah glanced up, desperately seeking Annie's help, a hand slapped her shoulder.

"Eyes on your work!" Miss Bradshaw snapped. "Daydreaming costs money."

The sharp sting shocked Sarah into frantic movement. She attacked the broken threads, trying to match the rhythm of the more experienced girls. But the more she rushed, the clumsier she became. The cotton fibers scratched her fingers raw, tiny cuts opening across her fingertips, spots of blood appearing on the white threads.

"Bleeding on the cotton costs money," Miss Bradshaw hissed, suddenly behind her again. "Work through it."

Sarah bit her lip to stop herself from responding. She'd never felt so helpless, so incompetent. At St. Michael's, she'd been known for her quick hands and steady work. Here, she was failing spectacularly.

From the corner of her eye, she saw Annie glance over, her face worried. When Miss Bradshaw stalked to the far end of the room, Annie quickly stepped over and fixed three broken threads on Sarah's machine with lightning speed.

"Use your fingernails to pinch the thread," she whispered. "Don't pull too tight."

Before she could say more, The Hawk's hand came down hard on Annie's back.

"Helping others costs money, Parker!" The

woman's bony fingers dug into Annie's shoulder. "One more infraction and you'll lose today's wages."

Annie's face paled but she nodded. "Yes, Miss Bradshaw."

Sarah mouthed "I'm sorry" as Annie returned to her station, blinking back tears.

The hours crawled by, and Sarah had never felt time move so slowly. The noise didn't fade into the background as Annie had promised it would. Instead, it seemed to grow louder, drilling into Sarah's skull until she wanted to scream.

Just when she thought she couldn't endure another second, a bell rang. The machines didn't stop, but the girls stepped away, replaced immediately by another shift of workers.

"Meal break," Annie said, appearing at Sarah's side. "We have thirty minutes. Come on."

Sarah tried to relax her hands, but they'd frozen into claw-like shapes from gripping the threads. She followed Annie through the maze of machinery, out into a small courtyard where workers sat on crates or directly on the ground, eating from small tins or cloth-wrapped bundles.

"I'm so sorry about earlier," Sarah said once they were outside, the cool air a blessed relief after the stifling heat of the spinning room. "I got you in trouble."

Annie shook her head. "It happens all the time. First day's the worst, but it gets easier." She tilted her head, examining Sarah's hands. "You're bleeding pretty bad."

Sarah looked down at her hands, surprised to see them covered in tiny cuts, "I'm fine," she lied.

"Next time, ask for help before The Hawk notices. She watches new girls especially close." Annie took a small bundle from her pocket. "I brought extra today. Figured you'd need it."

"You didn't have to…"

"Oi! Annie Parker!" a male voice called out. "Saving my seat like a proper lady?"

The boy from yesterday, Tommy Briggs strolled toward them, with a swagger in his step that seemed designed to irritate authority figures. His reddish-brown hair stood up at odd angles, and his blue eyes sparkled with mischief despite the dark circles beneath them.

"Tommy," Annie said, a blush creeping into her cheeks. "This is Sarah Dobbs. She's new."

"Tommy Briggs, at your service." He gave an exaggerated bow. "Also known as 'The Terror of the

Carding Room' and 'That Bloody Nuisance,' depending on who you ask."

Sarah couldn't help but smile. "Which do you prefer?"

"Depends on the day." Tommy dropped onto the ground beside them. "First day in spinning, eh? Tis Brutal. Your hands look like raw meat."

"Tommy!" Annie scolded.

"What? It's true." He dug into his pocket and pulled out a half loaf of bread and some cheese. "Here. Protein helps with healing. My aunt says so."

"I can't take your food," Sarah protested.

"You're not taking it. I'm offering." He broke off a large chunk of cheese and handed it to her. "Besides, it's all part of my cunning plan."

"What plan?" Annie asked suspiciously.

Tommy leaned in conspiratorially. "Feed the new girls, earn their eternal gratitude, build my army of devoted followers, then overthrow Thorne and take over the mill."

Annie rolled her eyes, but her smile betrayed her. "Ignore him. He thinks he's charming."

"I am charming," Tommy insisted through a mouthful of bread. "Tell her, Sarah. Am I not the most charming mill boy you've ever met?"

"You're the only mill boy I've ever met," Sarah pointed out.

"Then I win by default!" Tommy exclaimed triumphantly.

Sarah laughed. There was something irrepressible about Tommy Briggs, a refusal to be beaten down that she found instantly appealing.

"How was I supposed to know the storage room had a loose floorboard?" Tommy was saying, deep into what was clearly an embellished story. "So, half my body is stuck in the floor, Mr. Thorne comes down the hallway, and what does Jimmy Sutton do? He throws a sack over my head and tells Thorne I'm a new delivery of cotton bales!"

Annie giggled. "That never happened."

"Did too! I have the splinters to prove it," Tommy insisted, showing a scrape on his arm that could have come from anything.

The warning bell rang, signaling the end of their break. Tommy sighed dramatically.

"Back to the prison," he said, standing up and brushing off his trousers. "Sarah Dobbs, you survived your first morning. That's more than some can say."

"It's that bad for everyone?" Sarah asked.

"Worse for some," Tommy said, his joking

manner slipping for a moment. "Mills chew people up. Just ask Annie's…"

"We should get back," Annie interrupted quickly. "Miss Bradshaw will count us late if we're not at our stations when the machines restart."

Tommy gave Annie an apologetic look. "Right. See you ladies at supper, if the carding machine doesn't eat me first."

As he loped away, Sarah turned to Annie. "What was he going to say?"

"Nothing," Annie said too quickly. "Come on. If we're late, they dock half a day's pay."

The afternoon shift was, impossibly, worse than the morning. Sarah's fingers had stiffened during the break, and the cuts stung fiercely when she began working again. Miss Bradshaw seemed to hover constantly at her shoulder, criticizing her technique, her speed, her posture.

"Back straight! Shoulders down! Work faster!"

By the time the final bell rang, Sarah was nearly blind with exhaustion. Her arms felt weighted with lead, and her back like a column of fire. But it was her hands that troubled her most. They refused to uncurl from their spinning positions, locked into painful claws.

She and Annie stumbled back to the dormitory

along with dozens of other girls, no one having the energy for conversation. They ate a meager supper of thin stew and hard bread in the common dining hall before dragging themselves up the narrow staircase to their room.

"Let me see your hands," Annie said once they were sitting on their shared bed.

Sarah tried to extend her fingers but couldn't. The muscles seemed frozen.

"This happens to everyone at first," Annie said gently. "Here."

She took Sarah's right hand between her own and slowly began massaging the palm, working outward to each finger, gradually helping Sarah's hand relax and flatten. The process was painful, tears springing to Sarah's eyes, but she bit her lip and endured it.

"Thank you," Sarah whispered as Annie worked on the left hand.

"My cousin did this for me my first week," Annie said. "It gets better. Your hands toughen up."

"How long have you been here?" Sarah asked.

"Two years. I came from Bradford Workhouse after my parents died of fever." Annie finished with Sarah's hands. "There. Should be better by morning."

All around them, girls were preparing for bed,

changing into nightgowns, whispering quietly to avoid attracting Mrs. Pickering's attention. Sarah and Annie did the same, slipping under the thin blanket of their shared bed.

"Goodnight," Annie murmured, already half asleep.

"Goodnight," Sarah replied.

But despite her bone-deep exhaustion, sleep eluded Sarah. Her mind raced with the day's events, her body too sore to find comfort on the lumpy mattress. When Annie's breathing had settled, she carefully sat up and reached for her small bundle of possessions.

Hidden at the bottom, beneath her spare dress, was a slim book bound in faded leather. She'd taken it from the workhouse records room years ago, the blank pages at the back were her most prized possession after her locket. With painstaking care, she extracted a small pencil stub from the book's spine and opened to the first empty page.

The moonlight through the small window provided just enough light to see. Sarah positioned the book to catch the silvery light and began to write in tiny, neat letters.

*Tis my first day at Bailey's Mill. My hands won't work properly. The machine too fast. I fear they will fire me. If that happen where would I go? I won't be allowed back to St. Michael's and the thought of Madame Abbess doesn't sound appealing. How can this get better. How must I...*

"You can write?" Annie's whispered and it made Sarah jump. She quickly tried to hide the book, but Annie's hand on her arm stopped her. "No, don't. I'm not telling anyone. I just... I didn't know you could write."

Sarah hesitated, then nodded. "My mother taught me before she died. I practiced in secret at St. Michael's. If I didn't keep using it, I'd forget."

Annie stared at the book with something like wonder. "What does it say?"

"Just... my thoughts, about today."

"Could you..." Annie paused, glancing around to make sure the other girls were asleep. "Could you teach me? To read and write?"

Sarah blinked in surprise. "You want to learn?"

"More than anything," Annie said fervently. "My cousin was teaching me a little, before she..." She trailed off, then rushed on. "I know some letters. A few words."

One of the girls across the room shuffled in her sleep, turning over with a sigh. Annie and Sarah froze until the girl settled again.

"We'd have to be careful," Annie whispered, even more quietly than before. "If they find out you're educated, they'll put you on account keeping or supervisor training."

"Is that bad?"

"It's different work and it's away from us. They watch educated girls more carefully. Think they're more likely to cause trouble." Annie's eyes were serious. "Mill owners don't like workers who can read pamphlets about workers' rights."

Sarah considered this, then slowly nodded. "I'll teach you. When we can."

Annie smiled, her face lighting up with genuine joy for the first time since Sarah had met her. "Thank you."

As they settled back down to sleep, Sarah stared at the ceiling, thinking about Annie's warning. Being educated could bring unwanted attention, but it could also be power. Knowledge always was. Her mother had told her that, in the few memories Sarah still possessed of her.

*"Knowledge is the one thing they can never take from you, Sarah-girl. No matter how poor we are, no matter what happens, what you know belongs to you forever."*

## CHAPTER 4

Daniel

"This is the future of textile manufacturing, son." Edward Bailey swept his arm across the spinning room with the pride of a general surveying conquered territory. "Last year we added thirty new frames and doubled our output."

Daniel nodded, letting his father's boasts while he took in the reality before his eyes. The room stretched endlessly, crammed with machinery that clattered and banged with deafening insistence. Women and children scurried between the frames, their faces blank with exhaustion.

"How many machines does each worker manage now?" Daniel asked, noticing a young girl running between three different frames, her small hands moving frantically to tie broken threads.

"Three each on this floor. Used to be one per worker, but that was wasteful." Edward checked his pocket watch. "I had to make some efficiency improvements and production went up by twenty percent."

"Efficiency improvements," Daniel repeated. "You mean you're making them work triple for the same wages."

Edward's smile vanished. "Mind that tone, boy. These ideas you picked up at university won't serve you here."

"They are not just ideas, Father."

"I'm not interested in reform unless it means more money in our pockets," Edward snapped. "The workers should be grateful they have jobs at all."

A man in a worn supervisor's coat approached, tipping his cap nervously. "Mr. Bailey, sir. There's an issue with the new wool shipment."

Edward frowned. "What now?"

"Quality's not what was promised, sir."

"Damn it all." Edward turned to Daniel. "Look around if you must. I'll find you when I'm done."

Daniel watched his father march away, then turned back to the spinning room. Without Edward's dominating presence, he could observe more carefully.

The noise was worst of all. How did anyone think in this din? The cotton dust hung thick in the air, making his throat tickle after just minutes of exposure. He couldn't imagine breathing this for twelve hours daily.

Then he sat her. She was three machines from the end, a thin girl with dark hair pulled back in a neat braid. Unlike many others, whose faces showed only blank resignation, she seemed determined Instead.

She straightened, pressing a sleeve to her mouth to muffle the cough while her other hand continued tying broken threads. When she looked up, her eyes met his directly.

Daniel froze. Those eyes were clear hazel with flecks of gold and it held intelligence and a spark of defiance that struck him like a physical blow. She wasn't beaten down. Not yet.

The moment stretched between them. Then she turned away, back to her work, as if she'd never seen him.

A heavy hand landed on Daniel's shoulder.

"Found anything interesting?" Edward asked.

"Just observing the operations," Daniel said still watching the dark-haired girl.

Edward followed his gaze and chuckled. "Ah. I see. Well, a gentleman doesn't mix with mill girls, son. You're different breed entirely."

An older woman nearby dropped her shuttle with a clatter, her mouth tightening in disapproval.

"Time to go," Edward continued, oblivious to the reaction. "Your mother wants us home to prepare for the Harringtons' dinner tonight."

Daniel allowed himself to be steered toward the exit, but not before glancing back once more.

*** * * ***

"Daniel Bailey! How wonderful to see you again!" Catherine Harrington extended her hand with grace.

Daniel bowed over it slightly. "Miss Harrington."

"Please, you must call me Catherine." Her blue eyes sparkled with rehearsed charm. "After all, we've known each other since we were children."

That was stretching the truth considerably. They'd met perhaps three times at various society functions, but Daniel smiled politely.

"Catherine, then."

Mr. and Mrs. Harrington beamed at this exchange while Daniel's parents looked on with matching expressions of satisfaction. The six of them stood in the Harringtons' opulent drawing room, making small talk before dinner while servants circulated with drinks.

"Cambridge has certainly agreed with you," Catherine continued. "You look most distinguished."

"Thank you. You're too kind."

"Not at all! Your father has told us all about your academic achievements."

"Has he?" Daniel glanced at his father, who had cornered Mr. Harrington near the fireplace and was already deep in conversation about business.

Mrs. Harrington swooped in, taking Catherine's arm. "Dinner is ready. Shall we?"

The dining room gleamed with silver and crystal. Daniel found himself seated beside Catherine, with their parents across from them. A strategic arrangement designed to encourage conversation between the "young couple."

"Your father was just telling us about the mill expansion," Mr. Harrington said as the first course was served. "Tis quite impressive."

"Bailey's is the largest cotton mill in the county

now," Edward announced proudly. "And I expect it to be the largest in England within five years."

"With Daniel's help, no doubt," Mrs. Harrington smiled at him. "Such a fine young man. Cambridge educated and already learning the family business."

"Indeed." Edward raised his glass. "To the future of Bailey Mills."

Everyone drank, and Daniel managed a smile despite the knot forming in his stomach. The expectation in the room was suffocating.

"Catherine has been quite involved in charitable works," Mrs. Harrington said. "Tell Daniel about your committee, dear."

Catherine straightened, clearly pleased to have the spotlight. "I chair the Ladies' Committee for the Moral Education of the Working Classes. We believe that elevating the poor begins with proper spiritual and ethical instruction."

"How interesting," Daniel said carefully. "And what does this education entail?"

"Oh, we distribute pamphlets on temperance and virtue, organize Sunday readings of uplifting literature, and collect used clothes for deserving families." She leaned closer. "The poor desperately need guidance to improve their circumstances."

"And you find this effective?"

# THE MILL GIRL

"Absolutely! Last Christmas, we gathered twenty baskets of food for mill families. Such gratitude they showed! Though I must say, some seemed quite unappreciative considering their situation."

Daniel set down his fork. "Perhaps they were tired from working sixteen-hour shifts."

Catherine blinked, confused, before her smile returned. "It's important we teach them gratitude. But enough about my projects." She touched his arm. "Father says you're interested in mill operations. How unusual!"

"I believe understanding every aspect of the business is essential."

"Even the workers' conditions?" she asked, clearly puzzled.

"Especially those."

An awkward silence fell until Mr. Harrington cleared his throat. "Catherine, why don't you show Daniel the new patio garden? The night air is quite pleasant."

Catherine brightened. "What a lovely idea, Father!" She stood, offering Daniel her hand. "Shall we?"

Daniel had little choice but to follow her through the French doors onto a stone patio adorned with potted plants and wrought-iron furniture. Gas lamps cast a warm light over the scene, which might have been romantic under different circumstances.

"It really is wonderful having you back in Lancashire," Catherine said, settling onto a bench and patting the space beside her. "Society has been dreadfully dull without you."

Daniel sat, maintaining a proper distance. "I've only been gone three years."

"Three years is an eternity! Do you know how many balls and dinner parties I've endured with no interesting conversation?"

"I'm sure your many suitors provided entertainment."

She laughed, "None as educated as you. All they discuss is hunting and horse racing." She leaned closer. "I've always admired your intellect, Daniel."

"You barely know me, Catherine."

"But I'd like to." Her voice dropped to a conspiratorial whisper. "Our fathers have discussed our match for years. Didn't you know?"

"I suspected as much."

"And? What do you think of the arrangement?"

Daniel looked directly at her. "I think any marriage should be based on more than business advantages."

"Of course! There's also our social position to

consider." Catherine smiled, missing his point entirely. "The Baileys and Harringtons would make a formidable alliance."

"That's not what I meant."

"What then?" She frowned slightly.

"I believe marriage should involve genuine affection, shared values, and mutual respect."

Catherine relaxed. "Oh! How sweetly old-fashioned. You want a proper courtship before the engagement is announced. I completely agree."

"Catherine, I haven't agreed to any engagement yet."

Her smile froze. "Pardon?"

"I've only just returned home. I need time to settle into my role at the mill before considering marriage."

"But our fathers…"

"Our fathers can discuss business arrangements all they like. My personal life is my own affair."

Catherine's pleasant mask slipped momentarily, before she recovered. "Of course. How modern of you." She adjusted her approach, moving slightly away. "I respect your honesty, Daniel. It's refreshing."

Daniel softened his tone. "I mean no offense. You're a lovely young woman, but…"

"But you need time," she finished for him. "I understand completely."

She didn't understand at all, but Daniel saw no point in arguing further.

Catherine stood smoothly. "We should return before they send a search party." She offered a practiced smile. "I do hope we can be friends, regardless of what our fathers plan."

"I'd like that," Daniel said, though he doubted true friendship was possible with someone who viewed the world so differently.

As they walked back toward the dining room, Catherine slipped her hand into the crook of his elbow. "Just so you know," she murmured, "I'm perfectly willing to wait while you explore this... interest. Everyone needs a hobby before settling down to real responsibilities."

## CHAPTER 5

*S*arah

THREE WEEKS at Bailey's Mill had toughened Sarah's hands. The cuts had healed into calluses, and her fingers no longer locked into painful claws each night. She'd learned to tie broken threads, to duck from Miss Bradshaw's watchful gaze, and to breathe through the worst of the cotton dust without coughing.

She'd almost learned to ignore the constant hunger.

"Half-day today," Annie whispered as they

dressed in their Sunday clothes. "First one since you arrived."

Sarah buttoned her faded blue dress. It was her best and only good garment. "What should we do with such extravagant freedom?"

"Tommy wants to show us the meadows past town. He says the wildflowers are worth seeing."

"Wildflowers and fresh air? My, we'll be living like proper ladies of leisure."

Annie giggled, tying a worn ribbon in her blonde hair. "Mrs. Pickering would have fits if she heard you talking like that."

"Then it's fortunate she's busy terrorizing the new girls."

Sunday half-days were the mill workers' only taste of freedom, and even the most exhausted girls changed out of work clothes and whispered plans.

"Ready?" Annie asked, pinning her threadbare shawl.

"As I'll ever be."

They went down the narrow stairs and slipped past Mrs. Pickering's office, where the stern woman was lecturing a trembling new arrival. Outside, the air felt almost sweet compared to the mill's suffocating atmosphere.

Tommy waited by the gate, his hair combed for

once and his patched shirt cleaner than Sarah had ever seen it.

"Ladies!" He swept an exaggerated bow. "Your escort awaits."

"You look almost respectable," Sarah said.

"Don't tell anyone. I have a reputation to maintain." Tommy grinned. "Church first, then we have freedom."

The required Sunday service was held in a small chapel built by the elder Bailey for his workers, a fact the mill owner was never tired of mentioning as evidence of his Christian charity. The sermon, delivered by a minister who owed his position to Bailey, focused predictably on the virtues of hard work and obedience to earthly masters.

Sarah sat between Annie and Tommy, fighting sleep as the minister droned on about the rewards awaiting the patient servant in heaven. Tommy made faces each time the phrase "proper station in life" was mentioned, nearly causing Sarah to laugh aloud.

After the final hymn, they filed out with the other workers, past the watchful eyes of the overseers who took attendance. Missing church meant losing half-day privileges.

"That was uplifting," Tommy said when they were

safely away. "Nothing like being told poverty is God's plan to start the day right."

"Tommy!" Annie scolded, but her lips twitched.

"Where to first?" Sarah asked.

"Market's open till two. Then I promised to take you to meet my aunt."

They walked toward town, and for the first time, Sarah saw Lancashire beyond the mill walls. Streets bustled with Sunday shoppers, vendors called their wares, and children darted between stalls. The noise was almost as overwhelming as the mill but gloriously varied since it was human voices instead of mechanical clanging.

"Look!" Annie pointed to a stall selling ribbons and fabric scraps.

"Go on," Tommy said. "I'll wait here. Ribbon shopping exceeds my limited patience."

The girls browsed the colorful display while the vendor, a sharp-eyed woman with calculating smile watched them.

"This blue would suit you," Annie said, touching a faded ribbon.

Sarah checked the price and shook her head. "Too dear by half."

"How much for both this blue and the green?" Annie asked the vendor, surprising Sarah.

"Sixpence for the pair, not a penny less," the woman replied.

Annie dug into her pocket and produced the coins. "Done."

"Annie, you can't…"

"I can and I will." Annie handed over the money and tucked the ribbons into her pocket. "Happy three-week anniversary at Bailey's. You survived."

"I don't know what to say."

"Say you'll help me fix my reading later."

Sarah squeezed Annie's hand. "Deal."

They rejoined Tommy, who was watching a street performer juggle wooden pins.

"Successful shopping expedition?" he asked.

"Very," Annie said. "Where next?"

"Are you hungry?"

"Always," Sarah replied.

"Then it's time you met the formidable Mrs. Winters."

Tommy led them through winding streets to a small bakery tucked between a cobbler's shop and a laundry. A hand-painted sign reading "Winters' Baked Goods" hung slightly crooked over the door.

The shop was empty of customers when they entered, but the heavenly smell of bread made Sarah's stomach growl audibly.

"Tommy Briggs, is that you skulking in my doorway?" A stout woman emerged from the back room, flour dusting her apron and cheeks. "About time you visited your poor neglected aunt!"

"I've come bearing friends," Tommy said. "Aunt Bess, meet Sarah Dobbs and Annie Parker. They work in spinning."

Mrs. Winters wiped her hands on her apron and inspected them with shrewd brown eyes. "New lambs for the slaughter, eh? Bailey's always wants fresh ones." She shook her head. "Too thin, the pair of you. Sit down before you topple over."

Before they could protest, Mrs. Winters had ushered them to a small table and disappeared into the back. She returned moments later with a plate of buns and three mugs of tea.

"Eat," she commanded. "Day-olds, can't sell them anyway."

The buns were slightly stale but still delicious. Sarah tried to eat slowly, savoring each bite, but hunger won out.

"Good appetite at least," Mrs. Winters nodded approvingly. "Now, Tommy tells me you're from the workhouse? St. Michael's, was it?"

"Yes, ma'am," Sarah said.

"Horrible place. That Grimsby woman should be

locked up herself." Mrs. Winters sniffed. "Though Bailey's isn't much better from what I hear. Mr. Thorne's a right villain."

"Aunt Bess," Tommy warned.

"Oh, I know, watch my tongue." She waved dismissively. "But they should know what they're up against. Thorne has eyes like a hawk for pretty girls and he keeps a list of 'troublemakers' too."

Annie shifted uncomfortably. "He's always watching us."

"Of course he is." Mrs. Winters leaned forward conspiratorially. "Did you hear about Martha Jenkins? She worked in carding for six years, never a complaint. Then she asked for an extra break when her monthly pains were bad. Next day, gone! Thorne said she was 'stirring discontent.'"

"Aunt Bess is the town's unofficial newspaper," Tommy explained. "If it happens in Lancashire, she knows about it first."

"Someone has to keep track." Mrs. Winters poured more tea. "Just last week, Madge Taylor Caught her husband with the butcher's wife, right in their own bed! The nerve of some people."

For the next half hour, Mrs. Winters regaled them with town gossip, barely pausing for breath. She detailed the scandals of the mayor's wife who was fond of gin before noon, the church organist stealing from the collection plate, and the mill doctor prescribing the same useless tonic for every ailment.

"And don't get me started on the Bailey family," she continued. "Old Bailey treats his workers like cattle, while Mrs. Bailey pretends not to notice where their money comes from. And now the son's back, looking to take over someday. Heaven help us all."

"Have you met him? The son?" Sarah asked, surprising herself.

"Once when he came in for pastries." Mrs. Winters shrugged. "Polite enough, I suppose, but they're all the same when it comes down to it. Money changes how people see the world."

Tommy checked the small clock on the wall. "We should go if we want to see the meadow before heading back."

Mrs. Winters packed the remaining buns in a paper bag. "Take these. And Tommy, don't be such a stranger. Your poor old aunt gets lonely."

"You've never been lonely a day in your life," Tommy said, kissing her floury cheek.

"Cheeky boy. You two," she pointed at Sarah and

Annie, "Come back anytime, this one needs proper friends to keep him in line."

Outside, the sun had broken through the clouds, warming the usually gray town.

"Your aunt is wonderful," Sarah said.

"She's mad as a hatter, but I love her." Tommy slung the bag of buns over his shoulder. "Took me in after my parents died, even though she could barely feed herself."

"How did you end up at the mill?" Annie asked.

"Family debts. Father borrowed money he couldn't repay. When he died, Bailey offered to clear the debt if I worked for them until I turned twenty-one." Tommy kicked a stone. "Three more years to go."

"Then what?" Sarah asked.

"Freedom. Maybe I'll go to London or anywhere with possibilities." His usual cheeky grin returned. "But first, I promised you wildflowers."

They walked through town toward the outskirts, until the buildings gave way to open fields. The road less traveled was muddy from recent rain, but Sarah didn't mind. After weeks confined to the mill and dormitory, any excursion felt like an adventure.

"There." Tommy pointed to a sloping hill covered

in patches of yellow and purple. "Best view in Lancashire, which isn't saying much."

The meadow stretched toward a small stream, dotted with early summer blooms. In the distance, the mill's chimneys still belched smoke, but from here, they seemed less menacing.

Annie immediately began gathering flowers, weaving them into clumsy chains. Tommy sprawled on the grass, chewing a stem and watching clouds. Sarah simply stood, letting the breeze wash over her face, cleansing weeks of cotton dust from her lungs.

"We should come here every Sunday," Annie said, placing a crown of daisies on Sarah's head.

"Assuming The Hawk doesn't have us working," Tommy replied.

"Don't ruin it," Sarah said. "Just for today, let's pretend we're free."

They spent an hour in the meadow, talking and laughing with an ease impossible within the mill's oppressive walls. Tommy told outrageous stories about the carding room's characters. Annie taught them a clapping game she'd learned as a child and Sarah recited bits of poetry she remembered from her mother.

Eventually, the afternoon waned, and they reluctantly started back.

THE MILL GIRL

"Church bells," Annie noted as distant chimes rang out. "Must be afternoon service for the fancy folk who sleep late."

As if summoned by her words, a gleaming black carriage appeared on the main road ahead, drawn by matching bay horses. Even from a distance, the Bailey crest was visible on its polished door.

"Speaking of fancy folk," Tommy muttered.

They reached the intersection just as the carriage passed. Through the window, Sarah glimpsed Mrs. Bailey in a green silk dress, Mr. Bailey's stern profile, and beside him, the young man she'd seen watching her in the spinning room three weeks earlier.

This time, their eyes met for a fraction of a second before Tommy stepped forward and performed an outrageously servile bow, his nose nearly touching his knees.

"Your most grand and illustrious majesties," he intoned loudly. "How blessed we humble peasants are to breathe the same air as your exalted selves!"

Sarah couldn't help laughing, though she quickly covered her mouth. Annie gasped, torn between horror and amusement.

The carriage continued without slowing, but not before Sarah caught Daniel Bailey's startled expression and, unless she imagined it, the hint of a suppressed smile.

"Tommy! They'll sack you if anyone heard that!" Annie hissed.

"Worth it." Tommy straightened, grinning. "Did you see old Bailey's face? He turned purple like a plum."

"It's not funny," Annie insisted, though her lips twitched. "Sarah, tell him!"

But Sarah's laughter died as she spotted a familiar figure watching from the corner. Mr. Thorne stood motionless, his sour face unreadable as he observed them. When he caught Sarah looking, his thin mouth curved into what might have been a smile.

"We need to go," Sarah said quietly, nudging Tommy. "Now."

Tommy followed her gaze and swore under his breath. "He's making a list."

"And we're on it," Annie whispered.

## CHAPTER 6

*D*aniel

THE LANCASHIRE GRAND HOTEL'S private dining room reeked of cigar smoke and entitlement. Six men in expensive suits lounged around a polished mahogany table, with brandy glasses in their hand. Their combined wealth was enough to rebuild the city from scratch if they were ever so inclined.

Daniel sat beside his father, nursing a barely touched drink. He'd spent the past hour listening to these pillars of industry discuss production quotas and import taxes with the casual air of men selecting horses for a race.

"The Americans are undercutting us again," complained Henry Westmoreland, owner of three textile mills across Lancashire. "Their cotton prices are making us look like highway robbers."

"They don't have our labor costs," Richard Morton replied, swirling the amber liquid in his crystal glass. "No proper regulations over there."

Edward Bailey leaned forward. "Which brings me to my proposal, gentlemen. A coordinated adjustment across all our operations."

"Adjustment?" Morton raised an eyebrow. "How significant?"

"Fifteen percent reduction in wages," Edward said. "Across the board."

Daniel's head snapped up. "Fifteen percent?"

His father continued as if he hadn't spoken. "If we move together, the workers can't play one mill against another. They'll have to accept it."

The men nodded thoughtfully, and Daniel felt his stomach turn.

"Father, our workers already live on starvation wages. A fifteen percent cut would…"

"My son," Edward interrupted with a tight smile, "is fresh from Cambridge and full of economic theories. Please continue, Daniel. I'm sure these gentlemen would appreciate your university perspective."

The condescension in his voice was unmistakable. The other men shifted, some smirking, others examining their brandy with sudden interest.

Daniel hesitated, then pressed on. "I only meant that our workers can barely feed their families as it is. Many children at our mill show signs of malnutrition. If we cut wages further…"

"They'll tighten their belts," Morton interrupted. "It builds character."

"Perhaps they could eat their character for dinner," Daniel said before he could stop himself.

A moment of silence followed, broken by Westmoreland's bark of laughter.

"By God, Bailey, your boy's got fire in him!" He raised his glass. "To youthful idealism. May it survive contact with reality."

The others chuckled and drank. Daniel's father did not laugh.

"Why don't you take the carriage home, Daniel?" Edward's tone made it clear this wasn't a suggestion. "Tell your mother I'll be late. Arthur can return for me later."

"Yes, Father." Daniel stood, struggling to keep his expression neutral. "Gentlemen, good evening."

Their dismissive nods stung more than an

outright rejection would have. They'd already forgotten him, returning to their discussion of how best to implement the wage reduction.

Outside, the hotel doorman summoned the Bailey carriage. Daniel gave the driver his instructions, then settled into the leather seat.

As the carriage rolled through the streets, Daniel watched elegant shop fronts give way to crowded tenements and well-dressed ladies with parasols were replaced by gaunt women carrying heavy loads.

"Stop the carriage," Daniel called suddenly, spotting a crowd gathered in a small square ahead.

The driver pulled up, turning with concern. "Sir?"

"I'll walk a bit. Continue to the house and return for me in an hour."

"Mr. Bailey won't like…"

"An hour," Daniel repeated, already stepping down.

The crowd numbered perhaps a hundred, gathered around a makeshift platform where a man stood speaking. His clothes marked him as a mill worker, but he spoke with the conviction of an orator.

"They tell us to be grateful for our jobs," the speaker called out, "while they feast on the profits of our broken bodies! They call us lazy when we collapse after sixteen hours at the loom! They accuse us of theft when we ask for fair wages!"

Murmurs of agreement rippled through the crowd. Daniel moved closer, careful to keep his fine clothes from drawing attention.

"Bailey's Mill just hired twenty new children from the workhouse," the speaker continued. "Children who should be in school, now breathing cotton dust until their lungs bleed! And for what? So old Bailey can add another painting to his collection? Another thoroughbred to his stable?"

Daniel winced at the mention of his family name. The speaker wasn't wrong.

"We must stand together," the man urged. "United, we have power they cannot ignore. Divided, we remain at their mercy, and gentlemen like Bailey have no mercy to spare!"

The crowd cheered. Daniel found himself nodding along.

A woman near him noticed. "You agree, then?" Her gaze took in his quality coat.

"I do," Daniel replied simply.

"You're not from the mills," she observed.

Before Daniel could respond, a commotion erupted at the edge of the gathering. Police whistles shrieked, and uniformed men pushed into the crowd with batons raised.

"Disperse immediately!" an officer shouted. "This assembly is unlawful!"

Panic spread and people scattered in all directions as police charged the platform. The speaker jumped down, disappearing into the fleeing crowd.

Daniel backed away, torn between helping and staying anonymous. A young boy stumbled nearby, and Daniel caught his arm, helping him up before he could be trampled.

"Go that way," he urged, pointing toward a side street. "Quickly now."

As the square emptied, Daniel retreated to where his carriage would meet him. The encounter left him shaken. The speaker's words echoed in his mind, amplifying doubts that had plagued him since returning to Lancashire.

Had he really believed he could change things from within? His father and his colleagues had dismissed his concerns without a moment's consideration. What difference could he possibly make?

The Bailey household was in its evening rhythm when Daniel arrived home. Gas lamps glowed in windows, and the smell of dinner preparation

THE MILL GIRL

wafted from the kitchen. He handed his coat to the waiting butler and inquired after his mother.

"Mrs. Bailey is in her sitting room, sir."

Daniel nodded and headed upstairs, loosening his tie as he went. He needed his mother's after the events of the evening.

He approached her door, raising his hand to knock, when he heard a pained whimper from inside. He paused, then heard another sound. It was his mother's.

"Hold still, Lucy. I need to apply this properly."

Daniel pushed the door open without knocking. His mother knelt beside a young housemaid whose uniform sleeve was rolled up to reveal a badly burned forearm. The angry red skin was blistered and weeping, and the girl, no more than sixteen bit her lip to keep from crying out as Elizabeth Bailey applied some ointment to the wound.

Both women looked up in alarm at his entrance.

"Daniel!" His mother recovered first. "I didn't expect you back so early."

"Clearly." He closed the door behind him. "What happened?"

The maid, Lucy, glanced fearfully between them. Elizabeth patted her hand reassuringly.

"It's all right. My son can be trusted." She turned

to Daniel. "Lucy worked at the mill before coming into service here. Her arm was caught in a spinning frame three months ago."

"The doctor said it'd heal right up," Lucy said quietly. "But it hasn't, sir. It weeps and burns something awful."

Daniel looked more closely at the injury. Even to his untrained eye, the burn was severe and poorly healed, with signs of infection.

"The mill doctor told her it was nothing," Elizabeth continued, resuming her ministrations. "Sent her back to work the same day. When your father hired her for the house, she was still working her machine one-handed."

Lucy winced as Elizabeth wrapped clean bandages around her arm. "Your mother's been ever so kind, sir. I'd have lost the arm entirely without her help."

Daniel watched his mother work m, realizing this clearly wasn't the first such injury she'd treated.

"How many others have you helped?" he asked quietly.

Elizabeth secured the bandage before answering. "A few. When I can." She helped Lucy roll down her sleeve. "Take these willow bark tablets for the pain.

Come back tomorrow night, and we'll change the dressing."

"Thank you, ma'am." Lucy stood, bobbing a curtsy. "Sir."

When the door closed behind her, Elizabeth began cleaning up the medical supplies, avoiding Daniel's gaze.

"Mother," he said gently. "What you're doing…"

"Is what any decent person would do," she interrupted. "Nothing more."

"Father doesn't know, does he?"

Elizabeth's hands stilled briefly. "Your father has many concerns demanding his attention. There's no need to trouble him with household matters."

Daniel sat in the armchair opposite her. "How long have you been treating mill workers?"

A small smile touched her lips. "Since before you were born." She arranged bottles and bandages in a wooden box. "Your grandfather Bailey owned the mill first, you know. I was a debutante with no greater concern than which dance to attend." She closed the box with a decisive click. "Then I married your father and saw the mill."

"What happened?"

"I fainted dead away." Elizabeth laughed softly. "The noise, the heat, the children working those enormous machines. Your father was mortified. He didn't take me back."

"But you went anyway?"

"Not to the floor. But I met the wives and mothers who came to collect wages. Saw their burns, their crushed fingers, and their exhaustion." She looked directly at him. "What would you have done?"

Daniel didn't hesitate. "Exactly what you're doing."

"Then you understand why your father can't know." Her expression grew serious. "He believes in the natural order of things. Workers below, owners above, with no obligation beyond the wage."

"And you don't?"

Elizabeth sighed. "I believe we're all human, Daniel. Pain feels the same regardless of one's station."

Daniel leaned forward. "But you never said anything. Not to Father, not to me. All these years, I thought you agreed with him."

"What good would disagreement do? Your father built his life on certain principles. He won't change them now." She reached for his hand. "But you might build something different."

"Is that why you pushed me to learn the mill operations? To see for myself?"

Elizabeth smiled. "You always were quick."

"Father sent me home early tonight," Daniel admitted. "The mill owners are planning a coordinated wage cut. When I objected, they laughed."

"Of course they did." Elizabeth squeezed his hand. "Men like your father have never known hunger or cold. They can't imagine it."

"I saw a protest in town," Daniel continued. "The police broke it up while I watched and did nothing."

"You did the sensible thing. Getting arrested would help no one."

"But doing nothing helps no one either!" Daniel stood, pacing the room. "There must be something I can do, something more than sympathy."

Elizabeth watched him, with pride and worry in her eyes. "There's a group that meets at St. Mark's Church Hall on Thursdays. Factory reform advocates. Very respectable, doctors, lawyers, even a few progressive factory owners."

Daniel stopped pacing. "How do you know about them?"

"I have my sources." Elizabeth's eyes twinkled. "Lucy isn't the only one I help."

"Mother, you're a revelation." Daniel laughed, genuinely surprised. "All these years, I thought you were..."

"A proper society wife without a thought in her head?" She arched an eyebrow. "Your father made the same mistake."

"Does he know? About any of this?"

"Your father sees what he expects to see." Elizabeth rose, smoothing her skirts. "Now, you should change for dinner. And Daniel?"

"Yes?"

"Be careful. Small changes, made consistently, can accomplish more than grand gestures that burn out quickly."

Daniel nodded. "I'll remember."

As he turned to leave, Elizabeth called after him. "And Daniel? You might consider bringing Arthur when you visit St. Mark's. That boy sees everything and says nothing. Tis a valuable trait."

"How did you know I would go?"

Elizabeth smiled. "Because you're my son." Her expression softened. "And more like me than your father ever noticed."

Daniel left her room feeling lighter than he had in weeks. For the first time since returning home, he had an ally, and perhaps, a way forward.

## CHAPTER 7

## Sarah

IT STARTED with a tickle at the back of Sarah's throat. A minor irritation she ignored for days, washing it away with water during meal breaks. Then came the dryness, as if she'd swallowed sand, making each breath scratch like wool against raw skin.

By her fifth week at Bailey's Mill, the cough arrived.

"Everyone gets it," Annie said as Sarah doubled over during breakfast, her body shaking with each hacking breath. "The cotton dust settles in your lungs."

"Comforting," Sarah managed between coughs.

"Here." Annie pulled a small cloth from her pocket. "Tie this over your nose and mouth. Keep it damp. It helps a bit."

Sarah eyed the thin fabric. "The Hawk won't allow it."

"Just keep it loose around your neck. Pull it up when she's not looking."

In the spinning room, the air hung thick with floating cotton particles, visible in the shafts of light from the high windows. Sarah tied Annie's cloth loosely around her neck, positioning it for a quick pull-up when needed.

The cough worsened as the morning progressed. Each breath drew dust deeper into her lungs, and Sarah found herself fighting for air between fits. During a brief moment when Miss Bradshaw was occupied with a new girl, Sarah tugged the cloth up over her mouth and nose.

The relief was immediate. The damp fabric caught much of the dust before she inhaled it, and she could almost breathe normally again. She worked faster with proper air.

"Dobbs!" The Hawk called her. "What is that on your face?"

Sarah froze, her hands still on the threads.

"It's nothing, Miss Bradshaw."

"Remove it immediately."

"I just need…"

"Remove it or leave the floor." Miss Bradshaw's thin lips barely moved. "Your choice."

The other workers kept their eyes down, pretending not to listen, though Annie shot her a sympathetic glance from two machines away.

Sarah untied the cloth, stuffing it into her pocket. The dust rushed back into her lungs, and she fought to suppress another coughing fit.

"Masks slow production," Miss Bradshaw said, loud enough for nearby workers to hear. "You don't get paid to coddle yourselves."

She stalked away, and Sarah returned to her work, her eyes watering as she struggled not to cough. Just as she regained control, a loud snap echoed through the room, followed by the shriek of metal hitting metal.

Sarah's driving belt had broken, the leather worn through after years of use. The loose end whipped through the air, tangling in the spinning frame's gears. Metal ground against metal as the machine strained.

Workers in the room scattered as the frame shuddered violently. Sarah lunged forward instead of back, reaching into the moving machinery without thought. She grabbed the loose belt before it could wrap further around the gears, then yanked a lever to stop the frame.

The sudden silence was shocking. Every eye in the room turned toward her.

"What happened?" Mr. Thorne appeared at Miss Bradshaw's shoulder, his perpetual scowl deepening at the sight of the stopped machine.

"Belt snapped, sir," Sarah said, pointing to the frayed leather in her hand. "It was catching in the gears."

Thorne inspected the machine, his sour expression unchanging. "You stopped it?"

"Yes, sir. Then I extracted the belt before it could damage the mechanism."

He grunted, running his fingers over the gears. "The frame's undamaged." He seemed almost disappointed. "You know machines?"

"No, sir. Just... saw what needed doing."

Thorne exchanged a look with Miss Bradshaw. Some form of communication passed between them before he turned back to Sarah.

"We need a knotter in Section C. Jenkins, take over Dobbs' position. Dobbs, follow me."

Sarah glanced at Annie, whose eyebrows had shot up in surprise. Being pulled from the floor usually meant dismissal.

Thorne led her through the spinning room to a separate area where older women worked at small tables, to repair broken belts and tie complicated knots in thick ropes.

"Mrs. Fletcher, this is Dobbs. Show her the belt knots. She's yours now."

The oldest woman looked up, squinting at Sarah through thick spectacles. "Bit young for knotter work."

"She saved a frame," Thorne said, as if that explained everything. "Half penny more per day, Dobbs. Don't make me regret it."

With that, he was gone, leaving Sarah standing awkwardly before Mrs. Fletcher's table.

"Well, don't just stand there catching flies," the old woman said. "Sit. I'll show you proper sailor's knots, the only kind that holds in these machines."

Knotting work, Sarah discovered, was both better and worse than spinning. Better because she could sit occasionally, and the dust wasn't quite as thick in this corner. Worse because the constant manipulation of tough leather and thick ropes left her fingers bleeding again, reopening the calluses she'd developed at the spinning frame.

Still, the older women were a wealth of information. They'd worked at Bailey's for decades, and as their fingers worked, their tongues did too.

"Old Bailey's cutting wages again," Mrs. Fletcher muttered as she demonstrated a particularly complex knot. "Third time this year."

"I can't feed my grandchildren as it is," another woman agreed. "My daughter's taken in washing at night, just to buy bread."

"Young Bailey's different, they say," offered a third woman. "Educated and been asking questions about conditions."

Mrs. Fletcher snorted. "Don't fool yourself, Mary. He's his father's son. Might talk pretty, but when it comes to profits, they're all the same."

By late afternoon, Sarah's progress satisfied Mrs. Fletcher enough that she was trusted with a simple task.

"Take these repaired belts to the storage room," the old woman instructed, handing her a small stack of leather straps. "Ask Mr. Evans for three more of the heavy grade. He'll know what I mean."

Sarah nodded, grateful for a chance to stretch her legs. The storage room was on the mill's top floor, away from the noise and dust of the production areas. She climbed the narrow stairs slowly, her lungs still burning from the morning's exposure.

The storage room door was partially open. Sarah knocked lightly before pushing it wider.

"Mr. Evans? Mrs. Fletcher sent me for…"

She stopped abruptly. Instead of the storekeeper, Daniel Bailey stood by a shelf of ledgers, his shirt-sleeves rolled up with a pencil behind his ear. He looked as surprised as she felt.

"Oh! I'm sorry, sir. I was looking for Mr. Evans."

"He stepped out momentarily." Daniel set down the book he'd been examining. "You're from the spinning room, aren't you?"

Sarah nodded, suddenly conscious of her worn dress and dusty apron. "Yes, sir. Well, I was. I'm with the knotters now."

"A promotion?" His tone was genuinely curious

"Of sorts. Half a penny more per day to tie knots."

Daniel nodded, studying her with an intensity that made her uncomfortable.

"I should go. Mrs. Fletcher needs…"

"No, please. Stay." Daniel gestured to a chair. "Mr. Evans will return shortly. I was just leaving anyway."

An awkward silence fell between them. Sarah shifted her weight, uncertain what to do with her hands.

"Might I ask your name?" Daniel said finally.

"Sarah Dobbs, sir."

"I'm Daniel Bailey."

"I know."

His mouth quirked upward. "Yes, I suppose everyone here knows who I am."

He continued looking at her, and Sarah felt compelled to fill the silence. "Was there something else you needed, sir?"

"No, just..." He hesitated. "It's a pleasure to meet you, Sarah Dobbs."

"Not mutual," she muttered under her breath, then immediately regretted it.

Daniel's eyebrows shot up, and to her horror, he laughed, a genuine, surprised sound. "I beg your pardon?"

"I'm sorry, sir. That was inappropriate. I didn't mean…"

"No, please." He held up a hand, still smiling. "Don't apologize."

Before Sarah could respond, the door opened and an older man entered, carrying a box of supplies.

"Mr. Evans, there you are," Daniel said. "Miss Dobbs needs something from the storeroom. I'll leave you to assist her."

He nodded to Sarah, a strange half-smile still playing on his lips, and left.

Mr. Evans watched him go, then turned to Sarah with a raised eyebrow. "What can I help you with, miss?"

Sarah managed to complete her errand, though her face burned with embarrassment the entire time. What had possessed her to speak so rudely to the owner's son? She'd be lucky if she still had a job tomorrow.

\* \* \*

"Sarah Dobbs and Annie Parker!" Mrs. Pickering's yelled that evening. "You have a visitor waiting outside."

The girls exchanged confused glances. Visitors weren't allowed near the women's quarters after dark.

"Probably bad news," Annie whispered as they followed Mrs. Pickering down the stairs. "Someone's sick or…"

"Less chatter, more walking," Mrs. Pickering snapped.

To their astonishment, Mrs. Winters stood in the yard, a covered basket over her arm and Tommy hovering behind her like a lanky shadow.

"There you are!" Mrs. Winters exclaimed. "Thought that dragon would never fetch you. Come, I've brought supper."

Mrs. Pickering's lips tightened. "Thirty minutes, Mrs. Winters. Then they must return inside."

"Yes, yes, we know the rules." Mrs. Winters waved her away and led the girls to a bench near the mill wall. "Sit. You both look half-starved."

Once Mrs. Pickering disappeared inside, Mrs. Winters unveiled her basket with a flourish. "I brought leftover meat pies. I can't sell day-olds, you know."

The pies were still warm, and Sarah's mouth watered at the smell. Mrs. Winters pressed one into each of their hands, then a third into Tommy's already outstretched palm.

He devoured his in three massive bites.

"Good Lord, boy, slow down before you choke!" Mrs. Winters scolded

"Sorry, Aunt Bess." Tommy spoke through his last mouthful. "I missed dinner."

"Again? Why?"

Tommy shrugged, but Annie leaned forward. "Is that why you weren't at lunch? We saved you a crust."

"Mr. Thorne caught me helping Ben Wilkins with his carding. Said I was 'interfering with another worker's training.' Docked my pay and canceled my meal for the day."

"That's ridiculous!" Sarah exclaimed. "Ben's only eight. His arms barely reach the machine."

"Rules are rules." Tommy attempted his usual grin, though it didn't reach his eyes. "Worth it though. The little tyke was about to lose his fingers."

Mrs. Winters muttered something that sounded suspiciously like "murder" and "Thorne" in the same sentence.

"Calm down, Aunt Bess." Tommy patted her arm. "It's fine. I've still got three years to pay off my father's debt. I can't risk getting sacked now."

"Doesn't make it right," Mrs. Winters grumbled, then brightened artificially. "But enough about that miserable place. Sarah, Annie tells me you've been promoted to knotter. Moving up in the world, aren't you?"

"Hardly," Sarah laughed. "Just tying bigger knots for a half penny more."

"Every bit helps." Mrs. Winters handed her another pie. "Be thankful you are not the next Maggie Turner."

Tommy groaned. "Here we go."

"Hush, you." Mrs. Winters leaned forward. "She worked in the dye room for six years. Very pretty girl, but headstrong. She argued with Thorne once too often, and next thing you know, she's gone."

"Dismissed?" Annie asked.

"Worse." Mrs. Winters lowered her voice. "Ended up at Madame Abbess's house on Bridge Street. You know the type of establishment."

Sarah's stomach clenched. Matron Grimsby's had given a warning along the lines of *Get yourself dismissed, and there's only one place that takes ruined girls.*

"The docks are full of such places," Mrs. Winters continued grimly. "That's where girls without references end up. So you keep your heads down and your mouths shut, understand? No matter what you see or hear."

"We know," Annie said quietly.

"Good. I didn't bring you meat pies just to see you throw yourselves to the wolves."

"Don't worry, Aunt Bess." Tommy puffed out his chest. "I'll protect them."

Sarah laughed despite the serious conversation. "With what? Those twigs you call arms?"

"I'll have you know these are finely honed instruments of battle," Tommy protested, flexing his nonexistent muscles. "Shaped by years of hauling wool bales!"

"They look shaped by years of avoiding wool bales," Annie teased.

"The betrayal!" Tommy clutched his chest dramatically. "My own friends, mocking my magnificent physique!"

They dissolved into laughter, earning a disapproving glare from a passing overseer. Mrs. Winters shooed them behind a stack of crates until he passed.

Too soon, Mrs. Pickering rang the dormitory bell, signaling the end of their visit and Mrs. Winters packed up her basket, pressing the last pie into Tommy's hands.

"Come Sunday, if you can," she said, kissing Tommy's cheek. "I worry about you three."

After she left, Tommy walked the girls to the dormitory entrance. "She means well."

"She's wonderful," Annie said. "You're lucky to have her."

Tommy stepped back as Mrs. Pickering appeared in the doorway. "Night, ladies."

Back in the dormitory, as they prepared for bed, Annie nudged Sarah. "What happened today? In the storeroom?"

"What do you mean?"

"Mary from carding said she saw you talking to young Mr. Bailey."

Sarah felt her face warm. "I wasn't talking to him. Not really. I went for supplies and he happened to be there."

"And?" Annie pressed.

"And nothing. He asked my name. I told him. He left."

"That's all?"

Sarah hesitated, then admitted, "I might have been a bit rude."

"Sarah! To the owner's son?"

"It just slipped out." Sarah lowered her voice further. "I said meeting him wasn't a pleasure."

Annie's eyes widened comically. "You didn't!"

"I didn't mean to. It just... happened."

"What did he do? Was he angry?"

"No, he..." Sarah couldn't explain the strange moment between them. "He laughed."

Annie stared at her. "He laughed? At being insulted?"

"It was odd." Sarah shrugged, settling into bed. "But it doesn't matter. He's the owner's son and I'm a mill girl. Our paths won't cross again."

# CHAPTER 8

## Daniel

"Bailey, you magnificent devil!"

Daniel turned at the booming voice and found himself caught in a bear hug that lifted him clear off the ground.

"Will Norton. Still subtle as ever, I see." Daniel laughed as his friend set him down in the middle of Lancashire's Central Library. Several patrons glared at the disturbance.

William Norton had been Daniel's closest friend at Cambridge. He was brilliant, boisterous, and perpetually in trouble with university authorities for his radical newspaper articles. He was also the son of a Durham coal miner who had won his place through scholarship, a fact that made his friendship with the mill owner's son an unlikely one.

"Let's find somewhere quieter," Daniel suggested, guiding Will toward a reading alcove away from disapproving eyes.

"Your letter said urgent. Is everything all right?" Will asked once they were seated.

"That depends on your definition of 'all right.'" Daniel leaned forward. "What brings you to Lancashire? Last I heard, you were heading to London."

"I was. Plans changed." Will grinned. "I've taken a position with the Northern Review."

"The paper that keeps publishing those scathing articles about factory conditions?" Daniel raised an eyebrow. "My father burns each copy."

"Precisely the one." Will's expression grew serious. "They've commissioned a series on mill workers. I've got six months of research, interviews, and investigations."

"And you thought Lancashire was the place to start."

"Where better? The heart of the cotton industry, and home to the country's largest mills." Will's eyes gleamed. "Including the infamous Bailey's Cotton Mill."

Daniel winced. "Is that what they're calling it now? Infamous?"

"Your father has quite the reputation among the working class." Will pulled out a small notebook. "Which is partly why I wanted to see you. I need an insider's perspective."

"So, I'm a source now, not a friend?"

Will's face fell. "That's not what I meant. Look, I know it's your family business…"

"It's all right." Daniel waved off the apology. "Truth is, I've been hoping to talk to someone outside this echo chamber of mill owners. Someone who might actually care about what's happening."

"That bad?"

Daniel sighed. "Worse than I remembered. Children are working sixteen-hour shifts. The wages barely cover bread and my father and his cronies just agreed to a fifteen percent cut across all their mills."

Will whistled low. "They'll starve."

"They already are starving." Daniel rubbed his face. "There was a worker's gathering last week, but Police broke it up before it could gain momentum."

"I heard about that." Will scribbled in his notebook. "Any arrests?"

"A few. None from our mill, thankfully."

Will studied him. "You've changed, Bailey. The Daniel I knew at Cambridge complained about boring summers at his father's 'dreary factory.' Now you sound personally invested."

"I've seen things more clearly." Daniel hesitated. "Between us, I've been considering making changes when I eventually take over. Better conditions, and fair wages."

"Your father would hate that."

"Hence, 'eventually.'" Daniel smiled grimly. "But I need evidence, Will. Documentation of what's really happening, not just at Bailey's but everywhere. If I'm going to fight this system, I need ammunition."

Will tapped his pencil against his notebook. "I could use a source inside Bailey's. Someone who could provide details, numbers."

"Someone like me, you mean?" Daniel asked dryly.

"It would be anonymous, of course."

Daniel considered it. The risk was enormous because if his father discovered he was feeding information to a reform-minded journalist, he'd be disinherited immediately. On the other hand, how else could he enact real change?

"Let me think about it," he said finally. "I need to be careful. Not just for my sake."

"Your mother?"

Daniel nodded. "She's more vulnerable than she appears."

"Take your time." Will closed his notebook and slipped it into his pocket. "I'm staying at the Bull's Head Inn for the next month. Send a word when you decide."

They talked for another hour about their Cambridge memories and mutual friends before parting with a promise to meet again soon.

* * *

"The blue waistcoat, I think," Elizabeth Bailey said, inspecting Daniel's outfit critically. "It brings out your eyes."

"Is a waistcoat really necessary for a charity committee meeting?" Daniel asked, but dutifully changed as Arthur handed him the garment.

"Appearances matter in these circles," his mother replied. "Especially since Catherine Harrington will be there."

Daniel suppressed a groan. "I didn't realize this was another matchmaking attempt."

"Not at all. The committee does important work." Elizabeth smiled innocently. "That Catherine happens to chair is merely coincidental."

"As was Father's sudden business appointment preventing him from joining us?"

"Your father finds charity work tedious. You, however, expressed interest in the welfare of our workers. This seemed relevant."

Daniel couldn't argue with that logic. He finished dressing and offered his mother his arm. "Shall we, then?"

The Ladies' Committee for the Moral Education of the Working Classes met in the parish hall of St. Peter's Church, the wealthiest congregation in Lancashire. As they entered, Daniel noted the elaborate hats and fine dresses of the two dozen women arranging themselves around a long table.

Catherine Harrington spotted them immediately, rising from her seat at the head of the table with a wide smile.

"Mrs. Bailey! And Daniel, what a delightful surprise." She extended her hand. "Gentlemen rarely grace our humble committee."

"Daniel expressed interest in your charitable work," Elizabeth explained, taking a seat near the middle of the table. "I hope you don't mind his observing."

"Not at all! A man's perspective is always valuable." Catherine's smile brightened. "Perhaps you'll contribute some insights."

The meeting began with reports on various initiatives like moral instruction pamphlets distributed to factory workers, temperance pledges collected from reformed drunkards, and a program teaching basic housekeeping to working-class women. Daniel listened with growing discomfort as the ladies discussed the poor as if they were a different species entirely.

"Now, for our Christmas initiative," Catherine announced. "Last year's gift baskets were well received by the deserving poor. I propose we expand the program this year."

"Excellent idea," Mrs. Westmoreland agreed. "Perhaps add some warm clothing? The winter looks to be harsh."

"And moral literature," added another woman. "Improving stories for the children."

Daniel cleared his throat. "Might I make a suggestion?"

All eyes turned to him.

"Of course, Daniel," Catherine said warmly.

"The mill workers' children rarely have proper shoes. Perhaps we could include those in the baskets?"

A moment of silence followed.

"Well," Catherine said carefully, "our baskets are primarily for families showing moral improvement. The mill workers tend to be..."

"Less deserving?" Daniel asked.

"More difficult to reach," Catherine corrected smoothly. "Many spend their wages on gin rather than necessities. We focus our limited resources where they'll do the most good."

"But surely the children aren't responsible for their parents' choices."

Catherine's smile tightened. "We must consider the entire family unit. Those who attend our Sunday readings and demonstrate a desire for betterment receive our assistance. It encourages others to follow their example."

"So, help is conditional on attending your moral education sessions?" Daniel couldn't keep the edge from his voice.

"Daniel," his mother warned softly.

"We simply try to encourage proper values alongside material assistance," Catherine explained, as if to a slow child. "Giving handouts without moral guidance creates dependency."

Daniel bit back a retort about how the wages was so low that dependency was inevitable. "I see."

"Perhaps we should return to the matter of basket contents," Elizabeth suggested diplomatically.

The meeting continued, but Daniel had stopped listening. He watched Catherine direct the committee with absolute confidence in her moral superiority. She genuinely believed herself benevolent, even as she decided which poor children deserved shoes this winter.

The gulf between their worldviews stretched wider with each word she spoke. How could he ever have considered marrying someone so blind to the reality of working-class suffering?

After the meeting, Catherine cornered him as the ladies gathered their things.

"Your suggestion was well-intentioned," she said, touching his arm. "But charity requires discernment and not everyone can be helped."

"Or perhaps not everyone wants the kind of help being offered," Daniel replied.

Catherine's smile faltered. "I don't understand."

"I know." He softened his tone. "That's rather the problem, isn't it?"

Before she could respond, Elizabeth joined them.

"Catherine, the meeting was lovely as always. Daniel and I must be going, but thank you for allowing him to observe."

In the carriage ride home, Daniel stared silently out the window until his mother broke the tension.

"You're unusually quiet."

"I'm trying to find polite words for what I just witnessed."

Elizabeth sighed. "Catherine means well."

"Does she? Or does she simply enjoy feeling superior to those she 'helps'?"

"That's uncharitable."

Daniel turned to face her. "Those women sit in judgment of people whose lives they can't begin to comprehend. They offer moral instruction to children who haven't eaten since yesterday."

Elizabeth studied him carefully. "I knew you'd see it. That's why I brought you."

"You knew I'd be appalled?"

"I knew you'd understand the difference between genuine help and self-congratulatory charity." She took his hand. "Catherine will never change, Daniel. She's a product of her upbringing, just as you are of yours."

"I can't marry her, Mother."

"I know that too." Elizabeth squeezed his hand. "Your father will be disappointed."

Daniel laughed humorlessly. "Add it to his growing list. I've been thinking about what Will Norton said today... about exposing conditions at the mill."

"Be careful, Daniel." Her voice dropped. "I won't stop you from doing what you believe is right. But don't underestimate your father's reaction if you publicly damage the family business."

"What would he do? Disinherit me?"

"He might." Her eyes held a warning. "Or worse."

The carriage stopped at the Bailey mansion. Daniel helped his mother down, then paused.

"I think I'll skip dinner tonight. Tell Father I'm unwell."

Elizabeth nodded. "Where will you go?"

"The public reading room. I need to think."

The small library on the Bailey property had been established by Daniel's grandfather as a supposed benefit for workers, though its limited hours made it accessible to almost none of them. The standalone stone building had fallen into disuse, visited mainly by Daniel during his childhood.

He unlocked the heavy oak door and stepped inside,

expecting the usual musty emptiness. Instead, he found a slim figure hunched over a book at the single reading table, so absorbed she hadn't heard him enter.

Sarah Dobbs.

She wore the same worn dress he'd seen in the storage room, her dark hair neatly braided and pinned up. Her lunch, a small piece of bread, sat forgotten beside the open book.

Daniel must have made some noise, because she looked up suddenly, and her expression changed m to alarm in an instant.

"Mr. Bailey!" She stood quickly, nearly knocking over her chair. "I'm sorry, I didn't realize…I should go."

"No, please," Daniel said, gesturing for her to sit. "Don't leave on my account. I'm just surprised to find anyone here."

Sarah remained standing, clearly uncomfortable. "It's only open during lunch hour. Not many workers can spare the time to come, but I…"

"But you wanted to read." Daniel nodded toward the book. "What have you chosen?"

She hesitated, then turned the book so he could see the cover. "Dickens. Hard Times."

Daniel smiled. "Interesting choice. A novel about

factory workers and the industrialists who employ them."

"It seemed... relevant."

"Indeed." Daniel moved closer, careful not to seem intimidating. "What do you think of it so far?"

"I think Mr. Dickens understands more than most about mills like this one." She paused, then added quickly, "Not that I'm comparing Bailey's to Coketown, of course."

"Aren't you?" Daniel raised an eyebrow. "I would."

Sarah looked genuinely startled. "Sir?"

"Dickens got many things right. The dust, the noise, the deadening of the spirit." Daniel picked up the book, turning it gently in his hands. "Though I've always thought Bounderby more villainous than necessary. A caricature rather than a character."

"Some mill owners seem like caricatures themselves," Sarah said, then immediately pressed her lips together as if regretting the words.

Daniel laughed. "My father among them, I suppose?"

Her eyes widened. "I didn't say that."

"You didn't need to." Daniel handed the book back to her. "Please, sit. Finish your lunch. I didn't mean to interrupt."

After a moment's hesitation, Sarah sat down,

though she made no move to continue eating or reading.

"You're a knotter now, correct?" Daniel asked, taking the seat across from her. "How do you find it compared to spinning?"

"Better in some ways. Worse in others." She seemed surprised by his interest. "The dust isn't as bad, but the work is harder on the hands."

Daniel nodded. "I saw your hands in the storage room. The cuts had barely healed."

"You noticed?" Sarah looked down at her hands, now bearing new wounds from the rough rope work.

"I notice more than people think." Daniel leaned forward. "Like how you are here during your lunch instead of eating properly."

Sarah's chin came up. "Books feed the mind."

"While bread feeds the body," he countered. "Both are necessary."

"Says the man who's never gone hungry."

Daniel conceded the point with a nod. "Fair enough. Though I'd argue that's precisely why you should eat while you can and borrow the book for later."

"Borrow?" Sarah shook her head. "Books don't leave the reading room. Mr. Thorne's rules."

"Ah, but I'm a Bailey. Surely that counts for something in my own family's library."

A ghost of a smile touched her lips. "Are you suggesting I break the rules, Mr. Bailey?"

"I'm suggesting the rules are ridiculous." Daniel smiled back. "This library was meant to benefit workers, yet it's only open when most of you can't possibly use it."

"Most don't read anyway," Sarah said softly. "Or can't."

"But you can. Quite well, I'd guess."

"My mother taught me before she died… I practiced in secret at the workhouse. Would have been beaten if they knew."

"St. Michael's?" Daniel asked, remembering Mr. Thorne's reports on the new workers.

Sarah nodded.

"And now you're here, using your precious lunch to read Dickens instead of rest."

"Books are worth missing lunch for." Her smile grew, transforming her face. "They take you somewhere else, even if just for a few minutes."

Daniel found himself momentarily struck by that smile in an unexpected and genuine way.

"You have a lovely smile, Miss Dobbs."

The smile disappeared instantly, replaced by a frown. "I wasn't fishing for compliments, sir."

Daniel couldn't help laughing at her swift change of expression. "I never suggested you were. Tis just an observation."

She looked away, clearly uncomfortable with the personal turn in their conversation.

"I have an idea," Daniel said impulsively. "I have a rather extensive library at home. Many books gathering dust. What if I brought some here for you to borrow?"

"That's not necessary."

"But it is. Books should be read, not displayed." He grew more enthusiastic with each word. "I could leave them here for you. Any particular interests besides Dickens?"

"Mr. Bailey, I couldn't possibly…"

"Daniel," he interrupted. "Please call me Daniel when we're alone, at least."

Sarah looked scandalized. "That would be highly inappropriate."

"So is a mill owner's son having any conversation with a mill girl, according to my father. Yet here we are." Daniel shrugged. "If we're breaking one social rule, why not break another?"

"Because some rules carry greater consequences than others," Sarah replied.

Daniel sobered. "You're right, of course. Forgive me." He stood up. "But my offer stands. I'll bring books and leave them here. You can read them during lunch or...borrow them if you wish. No one checks this building but me."

Sarah hesitated, then nodded. "Thank you."

"What kinds of books do you enjoy?"

"Anything, really. Stories about places I'll never see. People living different lives."

Daniel felt a twinge at the matter-of-fact way she acknowledged the limitations of her world.

"I'll bring a selection tomorrow," he promised. "Leave them on this shelf here. No one need know they're specifically for you."

The lunch bell rang in the distance, signaling the end of the break. Sarah quickly gathered her things, wrapping the remaining bread in a scrap of cloth.

"I have to go," she said, returning Dickens to the shelf with obvious reluctance.

"Of course." Daniel stepped back to give her a clear path to the door. "Until tomorrow, then."

At the doorway, Sarah paused and looked back, meeting his eyes directly for the first time in their conversation.

Daniel smiled, unable to help himself. After a moment's hesitation, Sarah nodded once and was gone, hurrying back toward the mill.

Daniel remained in the reading room, contemplating the unlikely encounter. In the span of twenty minutes, Sarah Dobbs had shown more genuine intelligence and character than Catherine Harrington had demonstrated.

He ran his fingers over the copy of Hard Times she'd left behind, wondering what she'd make of the ending. Wondering, too, about the apparent coincidence that had placed her in his path not once now, but twice.

Perhaps not coincidence at all, but something else entirely.

# CHAPTER 9

*S*arah

SARAH HURRIED BACK to the mill, her mind still lingering on the unexpected conversation with Daniel Bailey. She slipped into the knotters' workroom just as the bell finished ringing, earning a suspicious glance from Mrs. Fletcher.

"Cutting it close, Dobbs," the old woman remarked, passing her a length of belt to repair.

"Sorry." Sarah settled at her workstation, trying to focus on the leather in her hands rather than the memory of Daniel's smile.

Annie appeared at the workroom door minutes later, her face flushed from running. She pinched Sarah as she passed to deliver thread to another knotter.

"Where were you at lunch?" Annie whispered on her way back. "I saved you half my bread."

"Later," Sarah murmured, conscious of Mrs. Fletcher's watchful eye.

The afternoon dragged endlessly, and when the final bell rang, she found Annie waiting outside the workroom.

"So?" Annie looped her arm through Sarah's as they walked toward the dormitory. "Where did you disappear to? And why were you so flushed?"

"I was not flushed," Sarah protested, touching her cheek. "I was at the reading room."

"For the entire lunch hour? With no food?"

"I had bread," Sarah defended, then changed the subject. "How was spinning today?"

"Dreadful as always." Annie coughed into her sleeve, a wet, rattling sound. "Don't change the subject. You've got a secret don't you?"

"A secret? Why do you say that?"

"You're not telling me something." Annie's eyes gleamed with mischief. "Is there a suitor I don't know about? One of the carding boys, perhaps?"

Sarah snorted. "Yes, Annie. I've been sneaking off for romantic trysts with Toothless Joe from carding."

"I knew it!" Annie clapped her hands. "Those three remaining teeth of his are simply irresistible."

They dissolved into giggles, earning disapproving looks from passing workers.

"What about you and Tommy?"

Annie's cheeks colored immediately. "We're just friends."

"Of course. Friends who blush at the mere mention of each other's names."

"I do not blush!" Annie protested, her face growing redder.

"Then you must be feverish," Sarah said, her smile fading as Annie coughed again, harder this time. "That cough sounds worse."

Annie waved off her concern. "It's nothing. Everyone has it."

"Not like that, they don't." Sarah stopped walking, studying her friend's face. "You're pale. And you're actually warm." She pressed a hand to Annie's forehead.

"It's hot in the mill. I'm fine."

But she wasn't fine. By bedtime, Annie was burning with fever, her breathing labored between coughing fits. Sarah slipped out of bed to wet a cloth

# THE MILL GIRL

in the washbasin, placing it gently on Annie's forehead.

"You don't have to fuss," Annie whispered.

"Hush." Sarah adjusted the thin blanket. "Try to sleep. You cannot afford to miss work because of me.."

"Try and rest first…"

They both knew mill rules: no work, no pay. And worse, missing two days meant possible dismissal.

Throughout the night, Sarah tended to Annie, replacing the cloth when it grew warm, helping her sip water between coughs. The other girls shifted restlessly in their beds, no doubt annoyed by the disturbance but too tired to complain.

The bell and the shuffling of exhausted girls preparing for another day came earlier than Sarah expected. Mrs. Pickering swept through the dormitory, barking orders until she reached Sarah and Annie's bed, where she stopped abruptly.

"What's this, then?"

"She's ill," Sarah said, standing to face the supervisor. "She needs a doctor."

Mrs. Pickering sniffed disdainfully. "Parker, can you work?"

Annie tried to sit up, only to be seized by another coughing fit.

"Obviously not," Sarah answered for her. "She has a fever. She needs medicine."

"Then she needs to see the mill doctor, who will determine if she's truly ill or merely malingering." Mrs. Pickering's thin lips compressed. "No pay for today, of course. And you," she pointed at Sarah, "are expected in the knotter's room at the bell."

"I can't leave her like this," Sarah protested.

"You can and you will." Mrs. Pickering's voice hardened. "Unless you prefer dismissal?"

Annie gripped Sarah's hand weakly. "Go," she whispered. "I'll be fine. I can go to Mrs. Winters..."

Sarah hesitated, torn between duty to her friend and the reality of mill life. One word from Mrs. Pickering, and she'd be on the street with no reference, and no way to help Annie at all.

"I'll check on you at lunch," she promised, squeezing Annie's hand before gathering her things.

Sarah's fingers worked, tying the knots only by muscle memory while her mind remained with Annie. When the lunch bell finally rang, she sprinted back to the dormitory, only to find Annie's bed empty.

"Where is she?" she demanded of a girl making her bed nearby.

"She went to the infirmary," the girl replied with a shrug.

The "infirmary" was a small room near the mill office where sick workers were kept until they recovered enough to work, or were dismissed. Sarah turned to leave, but Mrs. Pickering blocked her path.

"Back to work, Dobbs. No visitors in the infirmary."

"But…"

"Those are the rules." Mrs. Pickering's expression softened slightly. "The doctor's with her. That's more than most get."

Reluctantly, Sarah returned to the mill yard. With half her lunch break already gone, there wasn't time to eat. Instead, she found herself walking toward the small library.

A surprise waited for her there. Propped in the window seat near the back, partially hidden behind a curtain, sat a leather-bound book, just as Daniel had promised. Sarah glanced around the empty room before picking it up.

"Middlemarch" by George Eliot, with a folded note tucked inside the cover.

*Miss Dobbs,*

*This is a novel about provincial life, ambition, and the*

*gap between ideals and reality. I'd be curious to hear your thoughts when you finish.*

—D.B.

Sarah ran her fingers over the fine binding, far nicer than any book she'd handled before. She should leave it there. She knew that. His attention was dangerous, and the potential consequences severe. If Thorne discovered she was receiving books and notes from the owner's son...

But the temptation of being transported beyond Bailey's Mill for a few precious hours, was too strong to resist.

After a final glance around the empty room, Sarah slipped the book into her apron pocket. It made an obvious bulge, but her work smock would cover it until she reached the dormitory.

She managed three steps out the door before a commotion at the mill caught her attention. Workers spilled from the main building, gathering in confused clusters in the yard.

"What's happening?" she asked a passing girl.

"Three spinning frames broke down at once," the girl replied excitedly. "They're stopping production to check all the machinery. We've been sent back to the dorms until tomorrow!"

An unexpected half-day off would normally be

cause for celebration, but Sarah's first thought was of Annie. With the mill closed, she might finally get to the infirmary.

Those hopes were dashed when she reached the main building. Mr. Thorne stood at the infirmary door, turning away concerned friends of the sick.

"No visitors," he repeated firmly to each inquiry. "Doctor's orders. Back to your dormitories, all of you."

Sarah retreated, knowing better than to draw Thorne's attention. Instead, she returned to the empty dormitory, sat on her bed, and pulled out "Middlemarch." If she couldn't help Annie now, she could at least use this unexpected time to read.

She was fifty pages in when the dormitory door opened and Tommy's familiar voice called out, "Anyone home?"

"Tommy!" Sarah quickly hid the book under her pillow. "What are you doing here? You aren't allowed…"

"Relax. Mrs. Pickering's busy yelling at the new girls. No one saw me." He glanced around the empty room. "Where's Annie?"

"Infirmary." Sarah's worry returned in a rush. "Her cough's gotten worse, fever, too. They won't let me see her."

Tommy's usual good humor faded. "I just came from Aunt Bess's shop. She said to check on both of you."

"You've spoken to Mrs. Winters today?"

"Just now. I ran an errand for her during the machinery shutdown." Tommy shifted.

Something in his manner struck Sarah as odd. "You came straight from the shop?"

"More or less." He tugged at his collar. "Might've taken a detour."

Sarah studied him more carefully. His clothes were the same worn mill garments he always wore, but there was a new energy about him, a barely contained excitement.

"I've been hearing things, Tommy."

"What sort of things?" His voice was too casual.

"About your meetings. At the Bull & Whistle pub with some workers."

Tommy's eyes darted to the door. "Who's been talking?"

"People talk. Especially the older knotters." Sarah leaned forward. "Are you involved in something?"

"Maybe." A grin spread across his face, his restraint giving way to enthusiasm. "Actually, yes. And it's amazing, Sarah. Some workers are organizing across different mills, sharing information, planning…"

"Planning what, exactly?"

"Change!" Tommy's eyes gleamed. "We're not alone, Sarah. All across Lancashire, workers are saying enough is enough. No more wage cuts. No more sixteen-hour days. No more children labour."

Sarah glanced nervously at the door. "Keep your voice down."

"Sorry." He lowered his voice but couldn't contain his excitement. "There's a man, William Norton. He's a journalist and he's documenting everything. He's going to publish it in the Northern Review."

"And what good will that do?"

"Public outrage or political pressure, maybe" Tommy began pacing. "But that's just the beginning. Look at this." He reached into his pocket and pulled out what looked like a small block of wood with metal pieces attached.

"What is it?"

"My invention." He beamed with pride. "A quick-release mechanism for the power looms. If we install these on enough machines, we could shut down production in seconds. Makes it impossible for them to bring in replacement workers during a strike."

Sarah stared at the device, then at Tommy's

animated face. "That's sabotage, Tommy... you could be sent to prison or worse. Do you have any idea how dangerous this is?"

"Of course I do. That's the point." He sat beside her on the bed. "Someone has to fight, Sarah. If we all just keep our heads down, nothing ever changes. Is that what you want? For Annie to work until her lungs give out? For children to keep losing limbs?"

"Of course not, but..."

"But what? We should be grateful for our pitiful wages? Thankful they let us breathe their cotton dust until we choke on it?"

"It's not that simple." Sarah ran a hand through her hair. "What about your debt? Your aunt? What happens if you're arrested?"

Tommy's expression sobered. "I've thought about that. But what kind of man would I be if I did nothing while people suffered? While Annie got sicker?"

Sarah picked up the wooden device, turning it over in her hands. It was cleverly made, each piece fitting perfectly into the next.

"How many of these have you made?"

"Just the one so far. It's a prototype." Tommy took it back, tucking it safely in his pocket. "But if it works, we could make dozens."

# THE MILL GIRL

"And then what, we strike?"

"Eventually. When we're ready." Tommy's voice grew serious. "Promise you won't tell anyone. Not even Annie, not yet. She worries too much."

Sarah hesitated. Tommy's involvement in worker activism will put him in grave danger, but his passion was undeniable, and his arguments weren't wrong.

"I won't tell," she said finally. "But promise me you'll be careful. No unnecessary risks."

"Define unnecessary." Tommy's usual grin returned.

"I'm serious. These mill owners... are not just going to hand over better conditions because we ask nicely. You know what they're capable of."

"I know exactly what they're capable of. That's why I'm doing this." Tommy stood. "I should go before someone finds me here. Tell Annie I came by?"

"If they let me see her." Sarah walked him to the door. "Tommy? What you're doing... I understand it. I just don't want to see you hurt."

"Some things are worth getting hurt for." He glanced back at her, his expression uncharacteristically solemn. "Someday, you might feel the same."

## CHAPTER 10

Daniel

"I FAIL to understand why shooting defenseless birds constitutes entertainment," Daniel grumbled, standing stiffly as Arthur adjusted his hunting jacket.

"Because rich men need something to do between counting their money and drinking expensive brandy," Arthur replied deliberately deadpan.

Daniel's scowl cracked into a reluctant smile. "Careful. That borders on insubordination."

"It's merely an observation, sir." Arthur brushed Daniel's shoulders. "Besides, the Harrington shooting party is the social event of the season. Your absence would be noted."

"By my father, you mean."

"By your father, the Harringtons, and half of Lancashire society." Arthur handed Daniel his gloves. "Miss Harrington would be particularly disappointed."

Daniel sighed. "Catherine's disappointment is a price I'm increasingly willing to pay."

"Even at the cost of an argument with Mr. Bailey?"

"Even so."

Arthur studied him for a moment. "Your father already suspects you've lost interest in the match."

"My father suspects I've lost interest in everything he values." Daniel adjusted his collar. "And he's not wrong."

"Then perhaps today's event offers an opportunity." Arthur handed him his hat. "Show your face, fire a few shots, make polite conversation. It costs you a day but buys you time."

"When did you become so strategic, Arthur?"

"I've always been strategic, sir. It's why I'm still employed despite my frequent impertinence."

Daniel laughed then, the first genuine laugh since

his father had announced the shooting party three days ago. "What would I do without you?"

"Wear mismatched socks and alienate all of Lancashire society in a single afternoon, I expect." Arthur opened the door. "The carriage is waiting. Remember, a few hours of tedium now prevents weeks of paternal lectures later."

Carriages lined the circular drive of the Harrington estate as Daniel arrived, disgorging gentlemen in hunting attire and ladies in outdoor dresses who would observe from a safe distance.

Catherine spotted him immediately and broke away from a group of admirers to hurry toward him.

"Daniel! You came!" Her delight seemed genuine. "Father was certain you'd find an excuse to avoid us."

"I wouldn't dream of it," Daniel lied smoothly, accepting her gloved hand. "The weather's perfect for shooting."

"Isn't it? And the birds are plentiful this year." She slipped her arm through his, guiding him toward a gathering of young men examining shotguns. "You must meet my brother James. He's just returned from London."

Daniel had met James Harrington exactly once, years ago. He was a brutish boy even at sixteen, with his father's business acumen but none of his polish.

Now in his mid-twenties, James had grown into his frame, broad-shouldered and ruddy faced, with small eyes set too close together.

"Bailey!" James boomed, extending a meaty hand. "Heard you were back from university. Cambridge, was it? Waste of time, if you ask me. Education happens in business."

"I found value in both," Daniel replied, maintaining a pleasant expression despite the crushing handshake.

"Hah! Such a diplomatic answer." James turned to the men beside him. "Bailey here is father's pick for Catherine. Educated, wealthy, proper bloodline for grandchildren."

Catherine's cheeks colored. "James, really."

"What? It's hardly a secret." James clapped Daniel on the back hard enough to make him step forward. "Though I told Father he should have let you find a husband with more backbone. Bailey looks like he'd rather be reading poetry than shooting."

The men laughed, and Daniel forced a smile. "I guess I've got different pastimes for different occasions."

James lowered his voice conspiratorially, "I heard you've been showing interest in mill operations. Slumming with the workers, eh?"

Daniel stiffened. "I believe understanding all aspects of our business is essential."

"Only thing to understand about workers is how to keep them in line." James took a drink from a passing servant. "At our cotton mill, I make regular examples. Caught a girl sleeping at her post last month and had her publicly dismissed, blacklisted across Lancashire."

"How educational for her," Daniel said, his tone dangerously neutral.

James missed the warning. "They're like dogs, these people and need firm handling." He leaned closer. "Though some of the mill girls need handling of a different sort, if you understand me."

The men around him snickered.

"James," Catherine chided without real conviction.

"Oh, come now, sister. Every man here knows what I mean." James winked at Daniel. "Pretty young things with no options make for accommodating company. Bailey's probably sampled a few himself. I've seen some promising specimens."

"Actually, I haven't," Daniel said coldly.

"No? Your loss." James laughed. "Though I'm sure Catherine appreciates your restraint. Wouldn't want the future wife hearing about such diversions."

Daniel's hand tightened around his glass. "I don't view our employees as specimens for sampling."

"High-minded principles!" James laughed. "Give it time, Bailey. Once you've run the mill a while, you'll see them for what they are... tools for profit, nothing more."

The conversation veered into hunting territories then, but Daniel barely followed. His mind kept returning to James's casual cruelty, and the ease with which he discussed exploiting desperate young women.

When the group moved toward the shooting field, Daniel touched Catherine's arm. "I'm feeling rather unwell. Perhaps it's best if I excuse myself."

"Unwell? But you just arrived." Her disappointment seemed tinged with suspicion. "Was it something James said?"

"A headache, nothing more." Daniel forced a smile. "Please give your parents my apologies."

Catherine studied him, then nodded stiffly. "Of course. I hope you recover quickly."

Daniel was in his carriage within minutes, breathing deeply as it pulled away from the Harrington estate. James Harrington's words echoed in his mind, along with the laughter of men who saw nothing wrong with his attitudes. These were his peers, the men he was expected to associate with, to emulate, to become.

The thought made him physically ill.

The house was quiet when Daniel returned. He went straight to his room, needing solitude after the Harrington debacle.

A knock at the door interrupted his brooding. Arthur entered, carrying a familiar book.

"Sir, I collected this from the mill library as you asked."

"Middlemarch?" Daniel took the book. "Miss Dobbs returned it?"

"Yes, sir. I found it on the window ledge where you left the first one." Arthur hesitated. "There appear to be notes inside."

He opened it and discovered several small slips of paper tucked between the pages. The handwriting was neat but clearly unpracticed

*I like Mary best. She's practical and kind, and she reminds me of my friend Annie.*

*People here are just like Middlemarch, stuck in their ways, and suspicious of outsiders.*

*Dorothea thinks she can change everything. She's naive but brave.*

On the final page was a longer note.

*Thank you for the book. I've never read anything like it before. I stayed up too late reading.*

Daniel found himself smiling at her words. In their brief interactions, he'd sensed her intelligence, but these notes revealed a deep, thoughtful mind rarely given proper cultivation.

He selected another volume from his shelf. Charlotte Brontë's "Jane Eyre", and wrote his own note to tuck inside:

*Miss Dobbs,*

*Your observations on "Middlemarch" were fascinating. I particularly enjoyed your thoughts on Mary Garth. Perhaps you'll find Jane Eyre's determination equally compelling.*

*—D.B.*

He hesitated, then reached into his desk drawer for a small tin of healing salve his mother used. He'd noticed Sarah's cracked and bleeding fingers.

"Sir?" Arthur raised an eyebrow at the tin. "May I ask what that's for?"

"Miss Dobbs. Her hands were raw from the knotting work."

Arthur's expression remained neutral, but concern filled his voice. "May I speak freely?"

"When have you ever not?"

"Books can be explained away, but personal items

like a salve..." Arthur hesitated. "It suggests a different kind of interest."

"It's simple human decency."

"Perhaps to you. But how would it look to others? To your father? To her?"

Daniel sighed. "I know."

"Do you? Because a mill girl receiving gifts from the owner's son faces gossip at best. At worst, she could be dismissed."

"I hadn't thought of it that way," Daniel admitted.

"That's because you're thinking of her as a person, not the mill girl." Arthur's voice softened. "It's admirable, but dangerous for both of you."

Daniel reluctantly set the tin aside. "You're right."

"I usually am, sir." A hint of a smile touched Arthur's lips. "Though I take no pleasure in it this time."

Daniel removed the salve from the book but kept his note inside. "I'll be more circumspect."

"A wise decision." Arthur bowed slightly. "Shall I tell the kitchen you've returned? Your father is in the rear courtyard with Mr. Thorne."

"Thorne?" Daniel frowned. "Why is he here on a Saturday?"

"I believe they're discussing a personnel matter."

Daniel's interest sharpened. "I'll join them."

THE MILL GIRL

The courtyard has carefully tended flower beds surrounded by a stone fountain and wrought-iron furniture sat on a pristine brick patio. Edward Bailey and Mr. Thorne occupied two chairs with papers spread on the table between them.

"Daniel!" Edward looked up in surprise. "I thought you were at the Harringtons'."

"The party didn't hold my interest." Daniel nodded to Thorne, who half-rose from his chair. "Mr. Thorne."

"Mr. Bailey." Thorne's perpetual sour expression didn't change. "I trust you're well."

"Quite." Daniel took the third chair. "Don't let me interrupt your business."

Edward studied his son. "We're discussing a troublemaker at the mill. Thomas Briggs. The carding room boy."

"What's he done?"

"Nothing I can prove yet." Thorne's thin lips pressed together. "But he's been seen meeting with known radicals at the Bull & Whistle, labor agitators and that journalist from the Northern Review."

"William Norton?" Daniel kept his expression carefully neutral. "I knew him at Cambridge."

"Did you, now?" Edward's eyebrows rose. "What sort of man is he?"

"Passionate and a brilliant writer."

"He's been interviewing workers, collecting stories about so-called 'abuses' in the mills."

"So-called?" Daniel couldn't stop himself. "Are you suggesting these abuses don't exist?"

"I'm suggesting," Thorne said coldly, "that factory work is inherently difficult. Certain advocates exaggerate normal conditions to incite discontent."

Edward waved an impatient hand. "We're getting off topic. The Briggs boy. You're certain he's involved?"

"My informant is reliable." Thorne tapped a paper. "Briggs meets with them at least twice weekly. And he's been working on some kind of device."

"What device?"

"My source couldn't get close enough to see. But Briggs is clever with machines. Too clever for his own good."

"Hmmm" Edward's face darkened.

"Either way, he's a ringleader in the making. We should dismiss him now, before he causes real trouble."

Daniel frowned. "On what grounds? You've just said you have no proof of wrongdoing."

"We don't need specific grounds," Thorne replied. "His contract allows termination at will."

"Heaven forbid workers have rights," Daniel muttered.

"What was that?" Edward demanded.

"Nothing, Father." Daniel stood. "If you'll excuse me, I have correspondence to attend to."

# CHAPTER 11

Sarah

The workers of Bailey's Mill huddled together outside the chapel, their coats pulled tight against the chill. Sunday service had ended, but no one moved to leave. Mr. Thorne stood on the chapel steps, his perpetual sour expression even more pronounced than usual.

"By order of Mr. Bailey," he announced, "wages will be reduced by ten percent, effective immediately."

The crowd erupted. Men shouted and women gasped. Sarah felt Annie stiffen beside her.

"Ten percent?" a carding room worker yelled. "We can barely eat as it is!"

"My children haven't had meat in a month!" cried another.

Mr. Thorne held up a bony hand. "Silence! The decision is final. Anyone who objects can collect their papers and leave. There are plenty waiting for your positions."

Tommy pushed forward through the crowd, his face flushed with anger. "And where would we go? Every mill in Lancashire is cutting wages!"

"That's not Bailey Mill's concern," Thorne replied coldly. "The market dictates our decisions."

"The market doesn't have to feed our families!" Tommy shot back.

Thorne's eyes narrowed. "I'd watch that tongue, Briggs, unless you want to find yourself without employment entirely."

Sarah grabbed Tommy's sleeve before he could respond. "Not here," she whispered.

The crowd dispersed slowly. Sarah, Annie, and Tommy walked toward town, none of them speaking until they were well beyond the mill gates.

"Ten percent." Annie broke the silence. "That's nearly half my coal money for winter."

Tommy kicked a stone, sending it skittering

across the cobblestones. "It's not just about the money. It's how they do it with no warning, and no explanation, just 'earn less or leave.' Like we're nothing."

"We are nothing to them," Annie said softly. "Just parts of their machines."

"Only because we let them treat us that way." Tommy stopped walking, turning to face them. "This is exactly why we need to organize. The meeting at the Bull & Whistle tonight…"

"No." Annie shook her head. "Not this again."

"What would you have us do instead? Starve quietly?"

"I'd have us stay alive!" Annie's voice rose. "You think Bailey will just hand over better wages because we ask? They'll bring in workers from other towns, or use the police like they did at Marshall's Mill. Remember what happened there? Six dead!"

Tommy's jaw tightened. "So, you'd rather just accept whatever scraps they throw at us?"

"I'd rather not see you in prison! Or worse!"

"Stop it, both of you," Sarah interrupted. "Fighting each other is exactly what they want."

Annie and Tommy fell silent, both breathing hard.

"Look," Sarah continued, "Annie's right about the

risks. And Tommy's right about needing change. But right now, we need to figure out what ten percent less means for our daily bread."

"It means thin soup gets thinner," Annie said, rubbing her hands together against the cold.

"It means three more years of service becomes four," Tommy added bitterly, referencing his debt contract.

Sarah nodded. "Maybe Mrs. Winters will have ideas how we can get through this. She's lived through hard times before."

Tommy's face softened at the mention of his aunt. "She'll have a fit when she hears. Probably march up to the mill herself and give old Bailey an earful."

"I'd pay good money to see that," Sarah said, managing a small smile.

Annie linked her arm through Sarah's. "Well, let's not keep her waiting. Maybe she'll have day-old pies again."

"There's my Annie, always thinking with her stomach," Tommy teased, his anger momentarily forgotten.

Annie stuck out her tongue at him. "Better than thinking with my pride."

Mrs. Winters' shop was closed for Sunday, but

smoke puffed cheerfully from the chimney of the attached living quarters. Tommy didn't bother knocking, instead he pushed open the door and called out, "Aunt Bess! Your favorite nephew has arrived!"

"You're my only nephew, you daft boy," came the reply from somewhere.

Sarah and Annie followed Tommy inside, blinking as their eyes adjusted to the dim interior. Mrs. Winters' housekeeping bore no resemblance to the regimented order of mill life. There were books stacked precariously on every surface. Mismatched furniture crowded the space, and each piece was draped with colorful knitted blankets. A ginger cat slept peacefully in what appeared to be a bread bin.

"There you are!" Mrs. Winters came out from behind a towering pile of newspapers. She wore a flour-dusted apron over her Sunday dress, and her gray hair escaped its pins in wild abandon. "Just in time! I've made seed cake."

She pulled each of them into warm, floury embraces before ushering them to a round table covered with a lace cloth of dubious cleanliness.

"Sit, sit! I'll put the kettle on."

"Need help, Aunt Bess?" Tommy offered half-heartedly, clearly hoping she'd decline.

"From you? Last time you 'helped,' I found teacups in my flour bin for a week." She disappeared into her tiny kitchen, still talking. "How was church? Boring as usual? That new minister has all the personality of wet laundry."

Annie covered her mouth to stifle a giggle.

"Something happened after service," Tommy called after his aunt. "Bailey's cutting wages by ten percent."

A crash from the kitchen suggested Mrs. Winters had dropped something. She reappeared in the doorway, with a tea towel clutched in her hands. "Ten percent? Those thieving, black-hearted…" She unleashed a string of colorful language that made even Tommy blush.

"Mrs. Winters!" Annie gasped, though her eyes danced with amusement.

"Oh, don't 'Mrs. Winters' me. I'm too old to pretend." She returned to the kitchen. "In my day, workers would have marched straight to Bailey's fancy house and tipped his carriage into the pond."

Sarah exchanged a glance with Tommy, who mouthed, "Don't encourage her."

Mrs. Winters returned, balancing a tray loaded with cups, a chipped teapot, and a somewhat lopsided seed cake. "Here we are. Nothing fancy, but better than that slop they serve at the mill."

She poured tea into cups of wildly different sizes and designs. Sarah received hers in what appeared to be a repurposed jam jar with a handle glued to the side.

"It works just fine," Mrs. Winters said, noticing Sarah's inspection. "Why buy new when the old does the job? That's my motto."

"It's perfect," Sarah assured her, warming her hands on the makeshift cup.

Mrs. Winters cut the cake to produce slices of varying thickness. She pushed the largest toward Annie. "You need feeding up, girl. Still got that cough?"

"It's better," Annie said, though her slight wheeze suggested otherwise.

"Hmm." Mrs. Winters didn't look convinced. "I'll send you with some blackberry cordial."

They ate in silence for a few minutes. The cake was dense and sweet.

"Now then," Mrs. Winters said, setting down her cup with a decisive clink. "About these wage cuts. You'll need to stretch what you have. I can help with food when I can, but times are tight for everyone."

"We'll manage," Sarah said, though uncertainty gnawed at her stomach.

"Of course you will." Mrs. Winters' face brightened suddenly. "Oh! I nearly forgot! I've been practicing my tea leaf readings. Who wants their fortune told?"

Annie perked up immediately. "Me, please!"

"Drink up then, but leave a bit at the bottom."

Annie dutifully finished her tea, leaving just a small amount with the leaves. Mrs. Winters took the cup, swirled it three times counterclockwise, then upended it on the saucer.

"Now we wait for the leaves to settle," she announced, as if revealing a great mystery.

Tommy rolled his eyes at Sarah, who struggled not to smile.

After what Mrs. Winters deemed an appropriate interval, she lifted the cup and peered inside with exaggerated concentration. "Ahh! Most interesting."

"What does it say?" Annie leaned forward eagerly.

"I see... a bird! Yes, definitely a bird." Mrs. Winters rotated the cup. "That means a journey. And here, tis a circle of prosperity! And this shape here... well, that's clearly a heart."

"A heart?" Annie's cheeks colored slightly.

"Indeed! Romance is coming your way, my dear.

Someone close by who admires you greatly." Mrs. Winters darted a meaningful glance at Tommy, who suddenly became very interested in his cake.

"Your turn," Mrs. Winters said to Sarah, who had just finished her tea.

"I'm not sure I believe in fortune-telling," Sarah admitted.

"Nonsense! The leaves never lie." Mrs. Winters performed the same ritual with Sarah's cup, then gasped dramatically. "My goodness!"

"What?" Sarah leaned forward.

"A crown! That's very rare – it means success. And..." Mrs. Winters squinted theatrically. "A tall figure. A man of influence who will change your path."

Tommy snorted. "Let me guess. I've got a tall, handsome stranger in my future too?"

Mrs. Winters took his cup without asking and repeated her performance. "No, you have... a hammer. Hard work ahead. And a tree means growth. And most interestingly, crossed lines, which means important choices." She lowered her voice. "Choose wisely, nephew."

Tommy's smile faltered slightly.

Sarah watched Mrs. Winters' enthusiastic predictions with affection. The older woman might be embellishing, or outright inventing what she saw in the tea leaves, but her intentions were kind.

"More cake?" Mrs. Winters pushed the plate forward, oblivious to the cat that had now settled on a nearby stack of books, eyeing the seed cake with interest.

"We should probably head back," Annie said reluctantly. "Mrs. Pickering does bed checks on Sundays."

"That woman needs a hobby besides terrorizing young girls." Mrs. Winters stood, gathering plates. "Take the rest of the cake. And Tommy, come by tomorrow after work. I've mended your other shirt."

Outside, the afternoon had grown colder, a sharp wind cutting through their thin coats as they walked back toward the mill.

"Your aunt is wonderful," Sarah said to Tommy.

"She's something, all right." Tommy's expression turned serious. "Listen, about what I said earlier. The meeting tonight…"

"Tommy, please," Annie interrupted. "Not again."

"I'm just saying, if you change your mind…"

"I won't."

Sarah stepped between them. "Let's not start this again. We all cope differently. Tonight, I'm going to figure out how to make my soap last twice as long and darn my stockings for the third time."

"And I'm going to sleep," Annie added. "That's about all I can afford to do with ten percent less."

Tommy's shoulders slumped in defeat. "Fine."

They parted at the mill gates, Tommy headed toward the men's quarters while Sarah and Annie continued to the women's dormitory.

"You go on," Sarah told Annie at the door. "I want to... get some air before bed."

Annie gave her a curious look. "Everything all right?"

"Just restless. I won't be long."

Once Annie disappeared inside, Sarah turned and hurried toward the reading room. The small library sat dark and quiet, but the door was unlocked as always. Sarah slipped inside, her heart beating faster than the brief walk warranted.

Just as Daniel had promised, a new book waited in the window seat. She picked it up, running her fingers over the leather binding. "Jane Eyre" by Charlotte Brontë. A folded note fell from between the pages.

*Miss Dobbs,*

*Your observations on "Middlemarch" were fascinating. I particularly enjoyed your thoughts on Mary Garth.*

*Perhaps you'll find Jane Eyre's determination equally compelling.*

*—D.B.*

Sarah found herself smiling as she read his neat handwriting. The smile startled her, and she quickly schooled her expression, glancing around the empty room as if someone might have witnessed her reaction.

"Don't be ridiculous," she muttered to herself. "It's just a book."

Sarah noticed a small tin tucked into the book. Opening it revealed a sweet-smelling salve. She looked at her hands. The gesture was so unexpectedly thoughtful that her throat tightened.

For the past week, she'd worked late into the night, after Annie had fallen asleep, stitching a handkerchief by candlelight. Nothing fancy, just plain cotton salvaged from an old petticoat, but she'd embroidered a small flower in one corner, using the thread to carefully unravel it from the hem of her spare dress.

Sarah took it from her pocket now, smoothing the fabric with her sore fingers. It seemed a paltry offering compared to the books and salve, but it was the best she could manage. She placed it carefully where the book had been, tucking a corner under so it wouldn't blow away.

Settling into the window seat, Sarah opened "Jane Eyre" and began to read.

She was so absorbed that she almost missed the sound of footsteps approaching the library door.

## CHAPTER 12

*D*aniel

DANIEL STABBED at his roast pheasant, the angry clink of his fork against the plate punctuated his father's endless droning about production targets. Six servants hovered around the table, making the dining room feel crowded despite its size. The massive oak table, designed to seat twenty, made the three of them look lost in their own home.

"The wage reductions were announced today," Edward Bailey said between bites as if he was discussing the wallpaper. "Ten percent reduction across all departments."

"Ten percent?" Daniel set down his fork. "I thought the owners' meeting was set at fifteen."

"We compromised." Edward's smile didn't warm his eyes. "Seemed prudent to leave room for another cut next quarter."

Elizabeth Bailey's fingers tightened around her wine glass but she kept quiet.

"And this brings me to more pleasant news." Edward dabbed his mouth. "I've finalized arrangements with Harrington. The engagement will be announced next month at the summer ball."

Daniel froze mid-bite. "Engagement? My engagement?"

"Of course, your engagement. To Catherine Harrington." Edward continued eating as if he'd merely commented on the wine selection. "The legal papers are being drawn up. Harrington's textile imports combined with our manufacturing will create the largest textile empire in northern England."

"Father, I've not agreed to marry Catherine."

"You don't need to agree. It's decided." Edward waved dismissively. "The Harringtons are providing an exceptional dowry, and the marriage secures our social position."

"Our social position is secure enough without

selling me like a prize bull."

Edward's knife clattered against his plate. "Watch your tone, boy. This is business."

"It's my life."

"Your life is Bailey's Mill. It is your future, and your responsibility. This union benefits everyone."

"Except me," Daniel countered. "And Catherine, though she seems content to marry a stranger for status."

"Edward," Elizabeth interjected softly, "perhaps Daniel needs more time to…"

"I didn't ask for your opinion, Elizabeth," Edward snapped. "This matter is settled."

Daniel's jaw tightened. "Don't speak to Mother that way."

The table fell silent. Edward set down his utensils.

"I'll speak to my wife however I please." His voice dropped dangerously. "And you will marry Catherine Harrington as arranged. Your duty to this family supersedes your personal sentiment. Your grandfather understood this when he married. I understood it. Now it's your turn."

"And are you both so happy in your dutiful marriages?" Daniel looked at his mother, whose eyes stayed fixed on her plate.

"Happiness is a luxury," Edward declared. "Position, wealth, and legacy are all that matter. The engagement will be announced at the ball, with or without your cooperation."

Daniel stood abruptly. "Then you'll do it without me."

"Sit down!" Edward's fist hit the table. "We haven't finished discussing…"

"We've finished." Daniel tossed his napkin beside his plate. "I won't be part of this."

"Daniel," Elizabeth called softly as he headed for the door.

He paused, looking back at his mother. "I'm sorry, Mother."

Edward's face darkened. "If you walk out now…"

Daniel didn't wait to hear the threat. The dining room door closed behind him with a solid thud, cutting off his father's words.

He stormed through the house, past startled servants. Outside, the air cooled his anger slightly and like he was under a spell, his feet carried him toward the mill grounds and the small library building.

Daniel unlocked the door and stepped into the familiar smell of old books and dust. He didn't bother with the gas lamps, preferring the dimness as he dropped into a chair by the window.

Marriage to Catherine Harrington. The thought alone made his chest tight. It wasn't that Catherine was unpleasant, she was perfectly fine to chat with at parties. But to spend a lifetime with someone who thought charity meant giving moral lectures to the poor...

Something white caught his eye on the window seat. A handkerchief, small and plain but decorated with tiny flowers embroidered in one corner. He picked it up, running his thumb over the delicate stitching.

A sound behind the shelves made him turn and a book tumbled to the floor with a thud, followed by a gasp. Daniel rose, moving toward the noise.

"Hello? Who's there?"

Sarah Dobbs emerged from behind a tall bookcase, her face flushed. She wore her mill clothes, clutching "Jane Eyre" against her chest.

"I'm sorry," she said quickly. "I was reading and lost track of time. When I heard someone come in, I thought it might be Mr. Thorne."

Daniel couldn't help laughing at her mortified expression. "So, you decided hiding was the best option?"

"It seemed sensible at the time." Her lips twitched slightly. "I didn't realize it was you, Mr. Bailey."

"Daniel," he corrected automatically. "We've established that, at least in here, formality seems excessive."

Sarah bent to retrieve the fallen book, returning it carefully to its shelf. "I should go. It's late, and I've already broken enough rules for one day."

"You don't have to leave." Daniel held up the handkerchief. "I just found your gift."

She glanced at it, then away quickly. "It's nothing special. Just a thank you for the books."

"It's beautiful work." He traced the tiny pattern with his finger. "Especially considering mill work isn't kind to the hands."

"The salve will help." Sarah took a step toward the door, then hesitated. "Why are you here so late? If you don't mind my asking."

"Escaping, much like you." Daniel sank back into the chair by the window, suddenly tired. "Though I'm hiding from my family expectations rather."

Sarah remained standing, poised for flight, clearly uncomfortable with his candor.

"You can sit if you'd like." Daniel gestured to the other chair across the room. "I'm just going to read for a while."

After a moment's hesitation, Sarah perched on the edge of a chair near the bookshelf, as far from him as the small room allowed.

"Did you like 'Jane Eyre'?" Daniel asked, hoping to ease the tension.

"I've only just started." Sarah glanced down at the book in her hands. "But yes. Very much."

"Better than 'Middlemarch'?"

"It's different." She opened the book, marking her place. "Jane has a... directness I appreciate. She doesn't pretend to be something she's not."

"Unlike most people."

"Unlike most people with the luxury to pretend," Sarah corrected him.

Daniel smiled at her subtle rebuke. "Fair point. The working class has less opportunity for hypocrisy."

"Oh, we have plenty of hypocrites. They just lie about different things." Sarah relaxed slightly, her grip on the book loosening. "The mill is full of people who swear they'll leave someday but never do. People who talk of fighting the owners but bow and scrape when one appears."

"And where do you fall in this taxonomy of liars?"

"I try not to lie at all." She met his gaze directly. "Especially not to myself."

Something in her look made Daniel glance away first. "An admirable policy."

An awkward silence fell between them. Sarah opened her book again, apparently deciding that if he wouldn't leave, she might as well continue reading.

"That moment in 'Middlemarch' when Dorothea realizes her mistake," Daniel said suddenly. "Did you find it as satisfying as I did?"

Sarah looked up, surprised by the shift in conversation. "You mean her marriage to Casaubon?"

"Yes. When she finally sees him for what he is."

"I found it sad, actually." Sarah closed her book, giving him her full attention. "She wanted so badly to be part of something important, to help create something meaningful. Instead she found herself trapped with a man who resented her."

"You sympathized with her?"

"Of course. Don't you?"

Daniel considered this. "I always thought she was naive to marry him in the first place."

"Easy to say when you've never been a woman with limited options." Sarah said. "Though perhaps I shouldn't lecture the son of the mill owner about limited options."

Daniel laughed, surprised by her boldness.

"Touché, Miss Dobbs. Though I'd argue we all have constraints, just different kinds."

"Such as?"

"Social expectations. Family obligations. The weight of other people's futures resting on the decisions you make." He stopped, realizing he was revealing too much.

Sarah looked at him curiously but didn't press. Instead, she asked, "Who was your favorite character in 'Middlemarch'?"

"Fred Vincy," Daniel answered without hesitation.

"The perpetual student who gets into debt and causes trouble for everyone around him?" Sarah raised an eyebrow. "How surprising."

"He changes," Daniel defended. "He learns to take responsibility and finds work he truly values."

"With considerable help from Mary Garth," Sarah pointed out.

"We all need someone to believe in us when we're at our worst." Daniel smiled. "Even privileged troublemakers like Fred Vincy… What was the first book you ever read on your own?"

Sarah's face softened at the memory. "A tattered copy of 'Robinson Crusoe' that my father brought home. I was seven, and the workhouse took it when they took me. But I'd read it so many times I could recite whole passages."

"Is that how you survived the workhouse?"

"No one survives places like that unscathed." Sarah's expression grew serious. "But yes, having other worlds in my head helped."

"And now? What worlds do you prefer to visit?"

"Anywhere with people who speak their minds and face consequences bravely." Sarah's smile returned. "Though I also enjoy a good ghost story. The thrill of being frightened when you're actually safe is quite... luxurious."

Daniel laughed. "I have several excellent ghost stories in my library at home. Perhaps I'll bring one next time."

"I'd like that." Sarah glanced toward the small window, where the night had deepened considerably. "I really should go. Curfew was an hour ago."

"What happens if you're caught?"

"Mrs. Pickering will deliver a lecture on propriety, assign me extra chores, and possibly withhold breakfast." Sarah shrugged. "Nothing too dire, unless Mr. Thorne gets involved."

"He's that bad?"

"He has a ledger where he records infractions."

Sarah moved toward the door. "Three marks and you're dismissed without reference."

"And how many marks do you have?"

"None yet. I'm careful." She paused with her hand on the doorknob. "Though being found in a library with the owner's son after hours might earn me all three at once."

"I'd vouch for you."

Sarah laughed, a surprisingly light sound. "That would make it worse, not better."

Daniel rose too. "I'll check if the coast is clear."

He opened the door slightly, peering out into the darkened mill yard. "No one's about. You should be safe."

"Thank you." Sarah hesitated. "For the books. And the salve."

"Thank you for the handkerchief. And for talking with me." Daniel stepped back, giving her space to leave. "Though I suspect both were more than either of us intended to give."

"Good night, Mr. Bailey." She slipped through the door.

"Daniel," he corrected her retreating figure.

She glanced back once, a small smile on her lips. "Good night, Daniel."

# CHAPTER 13

Sarah

THE SUNDAY MORNING service dragged on, and the minister's lecture about respecting authority fell on deaf ears as Sarah mentally rehearsed her excuse to Annie. The final prayer seemed to take an eternity, but eventually the congregation shuffled to their feet for the closing hymn.

As they filed out of the chapel, Annie linked her arm through Sarah's. "Shall we go to Mrs. Winters' shop? Tommy mentioned she might have leftover tarts from yesterday."

Sarah hesitated. "Actually, I think I'll stay behind today."

"Stay? But it's our half-day." Annie's brow furrowed with concern. "Are you feeling ill?"

"No, nothing like that. I just want to catch up on some reading." Sarah nudged Annie gently with her shoulder. "Besides, you and Tommy should talk without me playing peacemaker."

Annie's cheeks flushed pink. "There's nothing to talk about."

"Isn't there? You've barely looked at each other all week." Sarah said. "He misses you. And don't pretend you don't miss him."

"He's being reckless," Annie whispered, glancing around to make sure no one overheard. "Those meetings of his will only lead to trouble."

"I know. But he's still Tommy and he's still the boy who brings you extra bread and makes you laugh."

Annie bit her lower lip. "What am I supposed to say to him?"

"Whatever you feel. Just talk to him." Sarah gave her a small smile.

"You're a terrible friend," Annie said, though her tone suggested the opposite. "Abandoning me like this."

"Absolutely dreadful," Sarah agreed. "Forcing you to spend time alone with a boy who adores you."

"He doesn't…"

"He does." Sarah gave her a gentle push toward the gate where Tommy waited, trying not to look like he was waiting. "Go on. Bring me back a tart if Mrs. Winters has any."

Annie took a few steps, then turned back. "Thank you," she said quietly.

Sarah watched her walk away, smiling at the awkward greeting between Annie and Tommy. His face lit up when he realized Sarah wasn't joining them, while Annie studied her boots as if they held great secrets.

The chapel emptied quickly, the workers were obviously eager to enjoy their brief freedom. Sarah waited until most had gone before heading toward the library. For the past three Sundays, she and Daniel had met there, sometimes reading side by side in silence, sometimes discussing books and ideas that had nothing to do with the mills or their class distinctions.

She'd come to look forward to these stolen hours more than she cared to admit.

Approaching the mill office building, Sarah slowed at the sound of raised voices from an open window and she heard Mr. Thorne's nasal tone.

"The new system will be implemented immediately. Half a day's wages for anyone late to their station. The same for talking during work hours or taking excessive breaks."

"And what constitutes 'excessive'?" asked a voice Sarah didn't recognize.

"Anything beyond the scheduled five minutes," Thorne replied. "Mr. Bailey's orders are clear. Discipline has grown lax and production is suffering."

"The workers won't like it," the other voice said cautiously.

"Their comfort is not our concern. Post the notice tomorrow morning," Thorne said with finality. "Any worker with three infractions will be dismissed without reference."

Sarah backed away from the window, her earlier anticipation replaced by a cold knot of anger. Half a day's wages for being a minute late or exchanging a word with a neighbor? With the recent ten percent cut, this would push many families from barely surviving to outright starvation.

The small stone building sat apart from the main mill complex, its windows catching the sun Sarah hesitated at the door, suddenly unsure. Perhaps she should turn back, find Annie and Tommy, warn everyone about what was coming.

Before she could decide, the door opened, and Daniel stood before her.

"Sarah." His smile was warm, genuine. "I was beginning to think you weren't coming."

"I almost didn't," she admitted.

His smile faded as he studied her face. "What's wrong? You look upset."

Sarah stepped past him into the library, pacing between the shelves. "I just overheard something interesting at the mill office."

"Oh?" Daniel closed the door, watching her with growing concern.

"Your father has implemented a new fine system." She turned to face him and crossed her arms. "Half a day's wages will be deducted for talking during work hours and for being a minute late or taking too long to use the privy."

Daniel's brow furrowed. "I hadn't heard about this."

"Of course you hadn't… Why would you? It's just another way to squeeze more profit from people who can barely feed their children as it is."

"Sarah, I don't control my father's policies."

"But you benefit from them." Sarah gestured

around at the library. "Every book here, every comfortable cushion, every meal you eat, all comes from our labor and our suffering."

Daniel took a step toward her and raised his hands in a placating gesture. "I know the conditions are harsh. I've been trying to understand, to find ways to help…"

"Help?" Sarah laughed bitterly. "Is that what this is? You lending me books while your family devises new ways to rob us? While your father treats his workers like equipment to be used up and discarded?"

"That's not fair," Daniel said quietly. "I'm not my father."

"Aren't you?" Sarah met his gaze directly. "You live in his house. You'll inherit this mill. You may feel sympathy for us now, but when it comes time to choose between your comfortable life and the consequences of change, which will you pick?"

"I'd like to think I'd choose what's right."

"So would I. But we both know what's likely." Sarah shook her head. "I should go. This was a mistake."

"Sarah, please." Daniel moved to block her path to the door. "Stay. Talk to me. Help me understand what I can do."

"Nothing. You can do nothing, because you are one of them, and I was foolish to forget it." She stepped around him. "Enjoy your books, Mr. Bailey. Some of us have to get back to reality."

"Sarah!" he called after her, but she was already through the door, walking quickly away from the library, from Daniel, from her own temporary delusion that friendship could cross the divide between them.

\* \* \*

THE WOMEN'S dormitory was in chaos when Sarah arrived later that evening. She had taken a walk by the river and threw stones across the water. Girls huddled in groups, whispering urgently, while Mrs. Pickering stood at the far end with a ledger in her hand. Sarah spotted Annie sitting on their bed, with her few possessions spread around her.

"Annie?" Sarah hurried over "What's happening?"

Annie looked pale as she looked up "They found a pamphlet in my apron pocket. About workers' rights."

"What?" Sarah sat beside her. "How?"

"Random inspection according to Thorne's new policy." Annie's voice was steady, but her hands trembled as she folded a worn nightgown. "They're dismissing me. I won't receive reference, and no final wages."

"That's not right! You can appeal to…"

"To whom, Sarah? Mr. Bailey?" Annie shook her head. "It's done. I have an hour to pack and leave the premises."

Sarah took Annie's cold hands in hers. "Where will you go?"

"I don't know. Maybe the textile factory in Oldham, though they prefer experienced weavers." Annie attempted a smile. "I'll manage. I always do."

"I'll share my wages until you find something else."

"You can barely feed yourself."

"We'll make it work." Sarah began helping Annie gather her sparse belongings. "I'm not letting you face this alone."

"Thirty minutes, Parker! I want you off the mill property as soon as possible." Mrs. Pickering yelled

Annie flinched but continued packing. "I should have stood my ground. I warned him to be careful."

"This isn't your fault."

"Isn't it? Tommy gave me that pamphlet as we came back a while ago. I should have burned it, but..." Annie trailed off, shaking her head. "I kept it.

Read it over and over and I imagined what it might be like if things changed."

Sarah lowered her voice. "Are Tommy's meetings organizing the workers?"

"That and more. They're planning something." Annie looked up, her eyes suddenly fierce. "Don't get involved, Sarah. Promise me. One of us without work is bad enough."

Before Sarah could respond, the dormitory door burst open. Tommy stood in the doorway, his face flushed from running.

"Tommy Briggs!" Mrs. Pickering strode toward him. "Men are not permitted in the women's quarters!"

"I need to speak with Annie," he said, ignoring the supervisor. "Please."

"You'll do no such thing. Leave immediately or I'll call Mr. Thorne."

Tommy's eyes found Annie across the room. "Two minutes. That's all I ask."

Mrs. Pickering opened her mouth to refuse, but Annie stood. "It's fine. I'm leaving anyway."

She walked past the other girls, head high despite their curious stares, and followed Tommy outside. Sarah grabbed Annie's bundle and hurried after them.

In the yard behind the dormitory, Tommy paced in agitated circles while Annie stood with arms crossed, her face unreadable.

"I'm so sorry," Tommy said when Sarah joined them. "This is my fault."

"Yes, it is," Annie agreed coldly.

Tommy flinched. "I never meant for this to happen. The pamphlet was just information. I didn't think they'd…"

"You never think, Tommy. That's the problem." Annie's composure cracked slightly. "I warned you. I told you they'd find any excuse to get rid of troublemakers."

"I know. You were right." Tommy stepped closer, reaching for her hand, but Annie pulled away. "Let me help you. I have some money saved. Not much, but enough to get you to Manchester maybe. Or you can stay with my aunt until…"

"I don't want your money. Or your help." Annie's voice quavered. "I trusted you, and now I have nothing. No job, no reference, no future."

"You have me," Tommy insisted. "We'll figure this out together."

"There is no 'we,' Tommy." Annie took her bundle from Sarah. "You chose your revolution over my warnings. Now I'm paying the price."

"Annie, please." Tommy's voice broke. "Tell me how to fix this."

"You can't fix it. No one can." Annie turned to Sarah, pulling her into a tight hug. "I'll write once I'm settled. Don't worry about me."

"At least go to Mrs. Winters," Sarah said, returning the embrace. "She'll help you figure out what to do next."

Annie nodded, then stepped back. "Be careful, Sarah. Keep your head down. And stay away from trouble." She cast a glance at Tommy, who stood miserably watching them.

"I will," Sarah promised, though the words felt hollow even as she spoke them.

Annie adjusted her shawl, squared her shoulders, and faced Tommy one last time. "Goodbye, Tommy. I don't want to see you again."

"Annie…"

"I've made my choice. You made yours too." Annie's voice hardened.

She walked away without looking back, a small figure carrying her entire life in a bundle no bigger than a pillow. Sarah watched until Annie disappeared through the mill gates, then turned to find Tommy staring after her, his expression stricken.

"She'll never forgive me," he said quietly.

"She might. Eventually." Sarah wasn't sure she believed it herself. "Once she's found her feet again."

"I never thought they'd go after her. She wasn't even involved." Tommy kicked at the ground. "It's not right."

"None of this is right." Sarah felt her earlier anger resurging. "And it's going to get worse with the new fines."

Tommy looked up sharply. "What new fines?"

Sarah told him what she'd overheard outside the mill office. Tommy's face darkened with each word.

"That's exactly why we need to organize," he said when she finished. "They think they can push us until we break. We have to show them we won't."

Sarah thought of Daniel in the library, his genuine confusion at her anger, his privilege to remain ignorant of decisions that devastated lives like Annie's.

"Maybe you're right," she said slowly. "Maybe it's time to push back."

Tommy stared at her in surprise. "You're serious?"

"Annie lost her position for having a pamphlet she never shared with anyone. What do we have to lose?"

"Everything," Tommy said, suddenly solemn. "You

need to understand that, Sarah. Once you're in, there's no going back."

Sarah thought of Annie walking away alone.

"I understand," she said quietly. "When's the next meeting?"

## CHAPTER 14

*D*aniel

DANIEL SHIFTED in his chair as Catherine Harrington detailed her vision for their wedding. The Harringtons had joined the Baileys for dinner, transforming what should have been a simple meal into an ordeal of endless courses and even more endless wedding talk.

"I've been considering June for the ceremony," Catherine said, patting her lips with a napkin. "The gardens will be in full bloom, and we can have an outdoor reception."

Daniel nodded, having given up on actual responses twenty minutes ago.

"The guest list is already at three hundred," she continued, undeterred by his silence. "Father insists we invite all his business associates, and Mother wants every family of consequence in Lancashire to attend."

"Three hundred?" Daniel finally spoke. "That seems excessive."

"Oh, it's not nearly enough!" Catherine laughed. "A Bailey-Harrington wedding is the social event of the decade. We simply must do it justice."

Mrs. Harrington nodded enthusiastically. "Catherine has been planning this since she was sixteen. She has a book filled with ideas… the flowers, the music, even the precise shade of ivory for her gown."

"How… thorough," Daniel managed.

"I've always believed in preparation," Catherine said, reaching across the table to touch his hand. Daniel resisted the urge to pull away. "And it gives us so much to look forward to."

"Indeed," Edward Bailey agreed, raising his wine glass to his lips.

Catherine launched into a detailed analysis of potential honeymoon destinations, each more elaborate than the last. Daniel found himself staring at his mother, silently pleading for rescue.

Elizabeth Bailey caught his eye and seemed to understand. She set down her fork. "Catherine, dear, I've just had the most wonderful thought. Would you like to see my winter conservatory? The night-blooming jasmine has just opened, and it's spectacular."

Catherine brightened immediately. "Oh, I'd love that! Mother, you must come too."

"Wonderful idea," Mrs. Harrington agreed, rising from her chair. "Perhaps Catherine can gather some ideas for her own conservatory... when you're settled, of course."

As the women left the room, Daniel exhaled slowly. "Thank you, Mother," he murmured under his breath.

With the women gone, Edward Bailey immediately turned the conversation to business. "James has some excellent ideas about expanding our shipping routes, Daniel. You should pay attention."

James Harrington, Catherine's older brother, leaned back in his chair with the confidence of a man accustomed to being heard. "I've secured exclusive rights to cotton shipments from three new plantations in the American South, with lower prices, and consistent quality."

"What about the American political situation?" Daniel asked. "There's talk of increasing tensions over slavery."

James waved a dismissive hand. "Business continues regardless of politics. The plantations will operate no matter who's in charge."

"Besides," Mr. Harrington added, "our concern is with cotton, not how it's produced."

"Precisely," Edward agreed. "Once we combine our businesses through this marriage, we'll control every step from raw material to finished product. Bailey's will manufacture, Harrington's will ship and distribute."

"A true empire," James said, raising his glass. "Nothing can stop us."

"We should also discuss the wage policies," Daniel interjected. "With the recent cuts and the new fine system, the workers are struggling to…"

"That's not dinner conversation," Edward cut him off sharply. "Besides, I've already explained our position on labor costs."

"But the new fine system is excessive. Half a day's wages for minor infractions…"

"Your son seems quite concerned with the help,"

Mr. Harrington observed, his tone suggesting this was a character flaw.

"It's a phase," Edward replied dismissively. "He has grand notions that haven't been tempered by real life experience."

James laughed. "I remember those days. I thought I could save the world too, until Father showed me the ledgers."

"Exactly," Mr. Harrington nodded. "Once Daniel sees how thin the margins really are, he'll understand the necessity of discipline."

"I've seen the ledgers," Daniel said quietly. "Our profits increased twelve percent last quarter, while the wages decreased by ten."

Everyone at the table did not say anything as Edward's face darkened. "You'll have to excuse my son, gentlemen. He's still learning the complexities of business management."

"No need for apologies," Mr. Harrington replied magnanimously. "Every young man goes through his rebellious period. Catherine will settle him down."

Daniel stood abruptly. "If you'll excuse me, I seem to have developed a headache."

"Daniel," Edward warned.

"Please extend my apologies to the ladies," Daniel

continued, ignoring his father's tone. "I think some air might help."

Without waiting for a response, he left the dining room, closing the door gently when what he really wanted was to slam it hard enough to rattle the china.

Instead of heading outside as he'd claimed, Daniel retreated to his study and closed the door. He poured himself a generous glass of brandy and drank half of it in one swallow, welcoming the burn.

A soft knock interrupted his brooding.

"Come in," he called, expecting his father's angry summons back to dinner.

Arthur Evans entered instead, carrying a small silver tray. "I thought you might want coffee, sir. For your headache."

Daniel smiled. "I doubt coffee is the cure for what ails me."

"Dinner did not go well?" Arthur set the tray down and began pouring coffee into a delicate cup.

"Catherine is planning our wedding down to the last flower petal, while her father and brother plot world domination." Daniel took the offered cup. "And my father encourages all of it."

"The Harringtons are an influential family," Arthur observed neutrally.

"The Harringtons are vultures in evening clothes," Daniel corrected. "James openly boasted about profiting from slave-produced cotton, and Mr. Harrington dismissed the workers as 'the help' as if they were furniture."

Arthur's expression remained carefully blank. "Most mill owners share similar views, sir."

"Including my father." Daniel set down his untouched coffee. "He implemented a new fine system without telling me. Half a day's wages for talking during work hours or being slightly late."

"I had heard about that," Arthur admitted.

"From the servants' gossip, I imagine?" Daniel raised an eyebrow.

"The staff does talk, yes." Arthur straightened a pile of books unnecessarily. "There's considerable anxiety below the stairs. The mill workers often have relatives in domestic service."

Daniel ran a hand through his hair in frustration. "What am I supposed to do, Arthur? I can't change my father's policies. I can't stop this ridiculous marriage arrangement. I can't even get through a dinner without wanting to upend the table."

Arthur hesitated visibly, his usual composure slipping. "May I speak freely, sir?"

"When have you ever not?" Daniel smiled wryly.

"More freely than usual," Arthur clarified.

"Please do. Someone should speak plainly in this house."

Arthur took a deep breath. "You talk about what you cannot do, sir, but I've yet to see what you will do."

"What do you mean?"

"You express outrage at dinner, you question your father in private, you read books about social reform." Arthur met his gaze directly. "But what actions have you taken?"

Daniel blinked, startled by the direct challenge. "I've been gathering information, and learning…"

"With respect, sir, the workers don't need your education. They need your influence." Arthur's voice remained quiet. "You know about William Norton's articles on mill conditions. You've witnessed the wage cuts firsthand. You've even spoken to the workers themselves."

"So what would you have me do? Publicly denounce my father? Surrender my inheritance and become a street revolutionary?"

"I would have you make a choice, sir." Arthur's formality returned somewhat. "Either accept that you are powerless to affect change, or accept the consequences of trying."

"That's rather stark."

"Reality often is, especially for those without the luxury of brandy and ability to make excuses."

Daniel stared at Arthur, seeing him clearly for perhaps the first time, not as his valet and childhood companion, but as a man with his own convictions. "You really believe I could make a difference."

"I believe you have a responsibility to try." Arthur adjusted his stance. "The workers respect you, sir. They've noticed your interest. Your name alone carries weight that someone like William Norton will never have."

Daniel was silent for a long moment. "You're right," he said finally. "I've been playing at concern without risking anything."

"I wouldn't put it quite that way, sir."

"But it's true." Daniel stood, suddenly energized. "I've been so careful not to offend my father that I've become complicit in his system." He paced the room.

"What will you do?"

"First, I need to speak with Norton. I can give him information about the wage cuts, the fine system, accident rates and maybe everything he needs for his exposé." Daniel turned to Arthur. "Can you get a message to him discreetly?"

"Of course, sir." Arthur's expression remained

neutral, but something like approval flickered in his eyes. "I know someone who knows someone."

"Tell him we need to meet. Soon." Daniel paused. "And Arthur? Thank you. For speaking freely."

Arthur allowed himself a small smile. "It's not often a valet lectures his employer."

"It's not often the valet is right." Daniel returned to his desk, pulling out paper and pen. "Now, I believe I have a letter to write."

As Arthur turned to leave, Daniel called after him. "This won't be easy. For either of us."

"Few worthwhile things are sir." Arthur paused at the door. "If I might make one more observation?"

"Please."

"Your father built his empire by being uncompromising. Perhaps his son might build something better the same way."

Daniel nodded slowly. "Let's hope so. Because after tonight, there's no going back."

## CHAPTER 15

*S*arah

THE KNOTTER'S room felt unusually hot that morning. Sarah tied another frayed belt, while her mind drifted between worry for Annie and regret over her confrontation with Daniel. Four days had passed without word from her friend, but Mrs. Winters had reported that Annie agreed to stay for a while with her.

"Did you hear about Annie Parker?" Bessie Wright whispered to Jane Morris at the next table. "She was caught with radical pamphlets. Probably got them from that boy she was sweet on."

"Tommy Briggs," Jane nodded knowingly. "I always knew she'd come to no good hanging around him."

"You wouldn't catch me risking my position for some boy's foolish ideas," Bessie continued. "Especially not one who talks big but does nothing."

Sarah kept her head down, focusing on the complex knot under her fingers, but her shoulders tensed with each word.

"Parker always thought herself better than the rest of us anyway," Jane added. "She was even trying to read books and such. What good did that education do for her?"

They snickered, and something in Sarah snapped. She turned to face them.

"Does it make you feel better?" she asked. "Mocking someone who's lost everything?"

The women stared at her.

"Excuse me?" Jane blinked rapidly.

"I asked if it makes you feel better. Or perhaps superior?" Sarah set down her work. "I'm genuinely curious. Does laughing at Annie's misfortune somehow improve your own situation? Does it add a penny to your wages or an hour to your sleep?"

Bessie flushed. "We were just talking. No harm in that."

"There's plenty of harm in it," Sarah replied. "Annie lost her job, her home, and her reputation in one day. And instead of showing an ounce of compassion, you're sitting here making her story more entertaining for yourselves."

Jane looked down at her hands. "We didn't mean anything by it."

"That's worse, isn't it? Being cruel without purpose." Sarah picked up her belt again. "If you're going to enjoy someone else's suffering, at least have the decency to admit it."

The women fell silent, returning to their work with chastened expressions. Mrs. Fletcher, the head knotter, gave Sarah an approving nod from across the room.

The moment of satisfaction was short-lived. A commotion from the far side of the room drew everyone's attention as Hannah Simms slumped forward onto her workbench, her face ashen.

"Hannah?" Mary Cooper shook her shoulder. "Hannah, wake up!"

The girl didn't respond. Mrs. Fletcher hurried over, checking her pulse.

"She's fainted. The heat's too much." She turned to the nearest worker. "Fetch water, quickly."

Before anyone could move, James Wilson at the

next table swayed dangerously and collapsed to the floor with a thud. Panic rippled through the room.

"What's happening?" Jane gasped, backing away.

A third elderly worker grabbed his chest and slid sideways off his stool.

"Someone get Mr. Thorne!" Mrs. Fletcher shouted, kneeling beside Tom. "And open those windows! We need air!"

Sarah rushed to Hannah, lifting the girl's head and loosening her collar. "She's burning up. We need to cool her down."

Workers crowded around the fallen, while others backed away in fear. Two overseers burst in, followed by Mr. Evans from the mill office.

"What's the meaning of this?" Evans demanded, surveying the scene with obvious displeasure.

"Three workers down, sir," Mrs. Fletcher reported. "Cause of the heat, exhaustion, and poor ventilation, I'd say."

"Get them to the infirmary," Evans ordered tersely. "And the rest of you, back to work. We're behind schedule as it is."

Sarah watched as Hannah and the others were carried out, their. The room temperature hadn't dropped, but no one dared open more windows without explicit permission.

"I wonder if they'll lose half a day's wages for fainting," Bessie muttered, just loud enough for Sarah to hear.

Work resumed in silence, like nothing happened. An hour passed, then two. At mid-morning break, Tommy Briggs appeared at the knotter's room door, his face flushed with excitement or nervousness, Sarah couldn't tell which.

"Quick word?" he beckoned to Sarah.

She glanced around to ensure no overseers were watching, then slipped over to the door.

"What are you doing here? This isn't your section."

"I'm making rounds," Tommy replied, pulling a folded paper from inside his shirt. "We're gathering signatures for a formal petition to Bailey about the wage cuts and the fine system."

Sarah stared at him. "A petition? That's your big plan?"

"It's a start," Tommy defended. "Norton from the Northern Review says we need documentation of our grievances and signatures to prove it's not just a few troublemakers."

"And you think Bailey will actually read this?"

"Whether he reads it or not, it exists as a record of our demands." Tommy glanced over his shoulder.

"Will you sign? We need as many names as possible."

Sarah hesitated, then nodded. "Give it here."

The petition was a surprisingly well-written document, listing specific grievances: the recent wage reduction, the excessive fine system, unsafe working conditions, and the lack of medical care. At the bottom, nearly thirty signatures already filled the page.

"Norton helped with the wording," Tommy explained, noting her surprise. "Educated-like, so they can't dismiss it as ignorant complaints."

Sarah added her name beside Eleanor Vance from the weaving shed. "How many signatures do you have so far?"

"Almost fifty across all departments." Tommy folded the paper carefully. "We're aiming for two hundred."

"Tommy!" Sarah warned suddenly, spotting movement in the hallway. "Someone's coming."

Tommy quickly tucked the petition back into his shirt as Mrs. Fletcher approached. "You shouldn't be here, Briggs. This isn't your section."

"Just passing a message to Sarah from Mrs. Winters," Tommy lied smoothly. "About Annie Parker."

Mrs. Fletcher's expression softened slightly. "How is the girl?"

"She's fine," Tommy replied. "Looking for new work."

"Shame what happened to her." Mrs. Fletcher shook her head. "Thorne's too quick with the dismissals these days. But you need to go, boy. Break's almost over, and Thorne's making his rounds."

As if summoned by his name, Mr. Thorne's thin figure appeared at the far end of the hall. Tommy paled.

"Go out the back," Mrs. Fletcher urged, pointing to the secondary exit. "Quickly now."

Tommy flashed her a grateful look and turned to leave, but Thorne had already spotted him. The overseer began walking in their direction, his perpetual frown deepening.

"Briggs!" he called sharply. "What are you doing away from your station?"

Tommy froze, his hand instinctively moving to protect the petition hidden beneath his shirt. Sarah saw the motion and knew instantly that Thorne would notice too since the man missed nothing.

Without hesitation, she grabbed the nearest shelf and gave it a hard shove. Three oil cans toppled over, spilling their contents across the floor with a splash. The slick liquid spread rapidly and the workers jumped back with cries of alarm.

"Clumsy girl!" Thorne barked, his attention immediately diverted to the growing mess. "What do you think you're doing?"

"I'm so sorry, sir," Sarah stepped forward, raising her hands in apparent distress. "I was reaching for my tools and lost my balance."

Tommy seized the opportunity to slip away, giving Sarah a quick nod of thanks before disappearing down the back stairs.

Thorne surveyed the damage, his thin lips pressed into a line of pure disgust. "Do you have any idea how much that oil costs, Dobbs?"

"No, sir."

"More than you make in a week." He pulled out his dreaded notebook. "That's half a day's wages for destroying company property."

"But sir, it was an accident," Sarah protested weakly, playing her part.

"Well accidents cost money and money comes from somewhere." Thorne scribbled in his book, then snapped it shut with finality. "Clean this up immediately, then report to Mr. Evans for additional duties after your shift."

"Yes, sir." Sarah ducked her head submissively.

As Thorne stalked away, Mrs. Fletcher appeared at her side with rags. "That was no accident," she murmured, low enough that only Sarah could hear.

"I don't know what you mean," Sarah replied, taking the rags.

"You've never been clumsy a day in your life, girl." Mrs. Fletcher gave her a long look. "Whatever Briggs is up to, be careful. Thorne's watching him, which means he's watching anyone who speaks to him."

"I'll be careful," Sarah promised, kneeling to sop up the oil.

"See that you do." Mrs. Fletcher glanced around, then added even more quietly, "Your friend Annie was just the beginning. Word is, Thorne has a list of 'agitators' he's looking to make examples of."

Half a day's wages gone, and additional duties after an already exhausting shift. The cost of her distraction was steep.

But as she cleaned the oil, she couldn't help wondering what the cost of silence would eventually be. How many more Hannah Simms would collapse before something changed? How many Annie Parkers would be cast out without reference or recourse?

Perhaps Tommy was right. Perhaps it was time

for all of them to sign their names and face the consequences together, rather than suffering them alone, one by one.

Sarah wrung out an oil-soaked rag and reached for another. One thing was certain, the neutrality she'd maintained was becoming increasingly difficult to justify, even to herself.

## CHAPTER 16

Daniel

Daniel sat at his desk, staring at the unread book beside his ledgers. Two Sundays had passed without Sarah appearing at the library. He'd waited both times, hoping she might return, but the small room remained empty except for her absence, which somehow took up more space than her presence ever had.

He tapped his pencil against the open ledger, and the neat columns of figures blurred before his eyes.

A knock interrupted his thoughts.

"Come in," he called, straightening in his chair.

Arthur entered, carrying a newspaper and wearing an expression Daniel had come to recognize as neutral.

"The Northern Review, sir. Today's edition." Arthur placed it on the desk. "I thought you might find page three of particular interest."

Daniel unfolded the paper. The headline jumped out immediately "EXPOSED: The Dark Secret Behind Bailey's Mill Prosperity." Below it, a smaller subheading read "Inside the Nightmare: Starvation Wages, Crippling Fines, and the Human Cost of Greed."

"He published it," Daniel murmured, scanning the article.

"Indeed, sir. Mr. Norton seems to have found quite a few sources."

The article detailed the recent wage cuts, the harsh fine system, and poor working conditions. It described children as young as eight working sixteen-hour shifts, workers fainting from heat and exhaustion, and families unable to afford both rent and food since the latest reductions.

Daniel recognized his own information woven throughout about the accident rates he'd copied from his father's records, details about the fine system he'd shared with Norton, even his description of the factory floor's poor ventilation. But what struck him most were the workers' direct accounts. There was a mother who'd lost two fingers in a loom and her job the same day; a child who worked with a fever because his family couldn't survive without his wages; a young woman dismissed without reference for possessing a pamphlet.

"I should mention that your father received a copy of the paper this morning as well."

As if summoned by his name, Edward Bailey burst through the study door without knocking, his face flushed with rage. He slammed a copy of the Northern Review onto Daniel's desk.

"Explain this," he demanded, jabbing a finger at the article. "Explain how this... this filth contains information only someone with access to my private records could provide."

Daniel met his father's gaze. "It appears to be an exposé on the working conditions at the mill."

"Don't play the fool. This trash contains our exact accident figures, production costs, wage calculations and details no outsider could know." Edward's voice dropped dangerously. "Details you reviewed just last month when I showed you the quarterly reports."

"Perhaps you should be more concerned with the

conditions themselves rather than who revealed them," Daniel replied.

"So you admit it? You betrayed your own family? You gave this Norton character our private information?"

Daniel glanced at Arthur, who retreated discreetly toward the door. "I think we should continue this conversation alone, Father."

Edward barely noticed the valet's departure, his focus entirely on his son. "Answer me. Did you provide information for this article?"

"I spoke with Norton, yes," Daniel said, setting the paper aside. "But every word in that article is true, which makes it an accurate report."

"The truth?" Edward laughed bitterly. "You naive boy. The 'truth' is that I've built something from nothing. I've built a business that employs hundreds who would otherwise starve. The 'truth' is that your education, your books, and your future comes from the mill you're so eager to criticize."

"I'm well aware of where our money comes from," Daniel said. "That's precisely the point."

"So, this is your rebellion? Feeding lies to some radical journalist with a grudge against my success?" Edward paced the small study. "Do you have any idea what this article will do to our reputation? The contracts it could cost us?"

"They're not lies, Father. Children are working themselves to death in our mill. Families can't feed themselves on the wages we pay. People are being dismissed without cause or reference."

"Those are business necessities, damn you. Every mill owner in Lancashire faces the same challenges."

"That doesn't make it right."

Edward stopped pacing to stare at his son. "Right? You think business is about what's 'right'? It's about survival. Profit. Growth. The moment sentiment enters the equation, everything collapses."

"Then perhaps it deserves to collapse," Daniel said quietly.

The room grew very still. Edward's face hardened into something Daniel barely recognized.

"You will issue a public statement," he said finally. "Disavowing this article. Calling it libelous fiction from a journalist with personal grievances against our family."

"I will not."

"You will, or you are no longer my son." Edward's voice was ice. "You will have no inheritance. No position. No place in this house."

Daniel's heart hammered in his chest, "Is that your final word on the matter?"

"It is." Edward straightened, adjusting his waistcoat. "You have until tomorrow morning to draft your statement. Arthur will deliver it to the paper."

"Then I suggest you begin looking for a new heir," Daniel replied. "Because I won't lie to protect a system that profits from suffering."

Edward's jaw tightened. For a moment, Daniel thought he might strike him. Instead, he turned toward the door.

"You're making a terrible mistake," he said without looking back. "One you'll regret when your principles don't keep you fed or clothed."

"Perhaps. But at least I'll be able to face myself in the mirror."

The door closed with a bang, and Daniel exhaled slowly. He'd known there would be consequences but facing them directly was another matter entirely. Disinheritance. Disownment. Everything he'd been raised to expect, gone.

He needed to think, to clear his head. And there was only one place he could do that properly.

The mill grounds were quiet as Daniel made his way to the small library. Most workers were in their dormitories, preparing for another week of labor.

The library was dark and silent, just as it had the past two Sundays.

To his surprise, a flicker of movement caught his eye as he approached. Someone was inside. He unlocked the door quietly and stepped in.

Sarah Dobbs stood by the window with a book in her hands. She looked up at his entrance, surprised.

"Mr. Bailey," she said formally, closing the book. "I was just leaving."

"Please don't." Daniel stayed by the door, giving her space. "I've been hoping you'd return."

"I shouldn't have come." She set the book down. "Our last conversation made it clear this was a mistake."

"I disagree." Daniel took a step forward. "I think this might be the only thing that isn't a mistake."

Sarah paused, studying his face. "You seem troubled."

"My father just threatened to disinherit me." The words came out with a laugh that sounded strange even to his own ears. "Apparently betraying the family business is an unforgivable sin."

"Betraying...?" Sarah's eyes widened slightly. "The article in the Northern Review. That was you?"

"Not just me. But I provided information, yes."

Daniel moved to the chair by the window. "Have you read it?"

"Tommy passed a copy around the knotter's room." Sarah remained standing, poised between staying and leaving. "It caused quite a stir. I recognized some of the accounts."

"I imagine Thorne is on a mission to discover the sources."

"He's already questioning people." Sarah hesitated, then sat in her usual chair. "Did you really risk your inheritance to help expose conditions at the mill?"

"It wasn't a calculated decision." Daniel ran a hand through his hair. "Norton needed information to verify what the workers told him. I had access to that information. It seemed simple at the time."

"Nothing about crossing your father is simple." Sarah's voice softened. "What will you do now?"

"Refuse to recant, I suppose and face whatever comes next." Daniel looked at her directly. "I've been thinking a lot about what you said, about benefiting from a system that causes suffering. You were right."

"I was angry."

"You were honest. And you made me see that sympathizing without acting is just another form of complicity." Daniel leaned forward. "I've spent years feeling uncomfortable with my father's methods while enjoying their rewards."

Sarah studied him. "I've heard stories. About you."

"Stories? Should I be concerned?" Daniel attempted a smile.

"Good stories. The workers talk about the young Mr. Bailey who actually looks them in the eye. Who asked about a child who lost fingers in the carding machine. Who arranged for a doctor when the mill physician dismissed a woman's injury." Sarah's eyes held his. "I reacted unfairly when I learned about the fine system. I blamed you for your father's actions."

"You had every right to be angry."

"Yes, but not at you. Not completely." She adjusted her skirt. "I came today to find another book. And perhaps to apologize."

"No apology needed." Daniel gestured to the shelves. "Though I'm glad you returned for the books, at least."

"The books," Sarah agreed, "and perhaps the company."

Daniel watched as Sarah traced the spine of "Jane Eyre" with one finger.

"Do you ever wonder what your life would be like if you'd been born into different circumstances?" he asked suddenly.

Sarah looked up. "You mean if I'd been born wealthy?"

"Or if our positions were reversed."

"You'd have died young, most likely. Working in the carding room or cleaning the machines is no small feat." Sarah's directness was refreshing after weeks of his father's politics and Catherine's social niceties. "Child mortality in the mills is impressively high."

"And you? If you'd been born a Bailey?"

"I'd have excellent posture, impeccable manners, and strong opinions about the proper way to pour tea." A small smile touched her lips. "Though I suspect I'd still love books."

"I think we remain essentially ourselves, regardless of circumstance," Daniel said. "You'd still be intelligent and forthright. I'd still question everything, much to everyone's annoyance."

"Some traits transcend class, perhaps." Sarah's smile faded. "But opportunity doesn't. Your questions are called intellectual curiosity. Mine would be called impertinence."

"Not to me," Daniel said quietly.

Their eyes met, and something shifted in the air between them. Daniel became acutely aware of how easily he could cross the small room, how little the distance was between them.

"I find myself looking forward to these conversations more than anything else in my week," he admitted. "Your perspective, and your honesty have changed how I see everything."

Sarah looked away first. "Mr. Bailey…"

"Daniel. Please."

"Daniel." The word seemed to cost her something. "Whatever you're trying to say, I think you should consider carefully before saying it."

"I'm saying I value your company. Your mind. Your..." He trailed off, searching for words that wouldn't frighten her away. "Friendship, if I could be so presumptuous."

"Friendship." Sarah repeated the word as if testing its weight. "Is that what this is?"

"What would you call it?"

"Complicated." She stood, replacing "Jane Eyre" on the shelf. "And likely to become more so."

"Because of our different positions?"

"Because you're still a Bailey, disinherited or not. And I'm still a mill girl with no prospects beyond these walls." Sarah turned to face him. "Some boundaries can't be crossed without consequences for everyone involved."

"Sarah…"

"I should go." She moved toward the door. "Mrs. Pickering will be checking the dormitories soon."

Daniel stood too. "Will you come back next Sunday?"

Sarah paused, her hand on the doorknob. "That would be unwise."

"Probably. Most of my recent decisions have been." Daniel smiled ruefully. "But I'd like to see you again."

"Good night, Daniel." Sarah slipped through the door before he could respond.

## CHAPTER 17

### Sarah

Sarah replayed yesterday's conversation with Daniel. The memory of his face when he'd almost said more than "friendship" troubled her more than she cared to admit.

Mrs. Fletcher appeared at her workbench, "Sarah. Mr. Thorne wants to see you."

The room went quiet. Being summoned by Thorne never ended well.

"Did he say why?" Sarah set down her work, wiping her hands on her apron.

"No. But he's waiting at the office." Mrs. Fletcher

lowered her voice. "Straighten your collar and mind your tongue."

Sarah's stomach tightened as she followed the older woman through the mill. Outside Thorne's office, Mrs. Fletcher gave her a small nod before returning to the knotter's room.

Sarah knocked.

"Enter,"

He sat at his desk, his sour expression particularly pronounced today. To Sarah's surprise, a well-dressed man she didn't recognize stood by the window.

"Dobbs," Thorne said without preamble. "This is Mr. Rhodes, Mr. Bailey's personal secretary. He has a message for you."

Mr. Rhodes stepped forward. "Miss Dobbs. Mr. Edward Bailey requests your presence at the main house immediately."

Sarah blinked. "The main house? Whatever for?"

"It's not your place to question," Thorne cut in. "Mr. Bailey doesn't summon mill girls without reason."

"I'm to escort you," Rhodes said, checking his pocket watch. "Mr. Bailey's time is valuable."

"Now? But my work…"

"Has been excused for the morning," Thorne finished. "Go with Mr. Rhodes."

Sarah had no choice but to follow the secretary out of the mill. Walking through the yard felt surreal because leaving during working hours without being dismissed was unprecedented. Workers stared from windows as she passed.

"Why does Mr. Bailey want to see me?" she tried again as they approached the imposing Bailey mansion.

"That's Mr. Bailey's business," Rhodes replied without looking at her. "Though I understand it concerns a position."

"A position?"

Rhodes didn't elaborate, leading her through the servant's entrance at the rear of the house. The kitchen staff looked up in surprise as they passed through, a young maid nearly dropping the platter she carried.

Sarah had never been inside the Bailey home. Its grandeur struck her immediately. It's had gleaming wood, expensive fabrics, and spaciousness utterly foreign to someone raised in workhouses and dormitories. This single house could comfortably fit thirty mill families or more.

Rhodes stopped at a heavy oak door, knocking

twice before opening it. "Miss Dobbs, sir, as requested."

Edward Bailey sat behind a massive desk, with papers arranged in precise stacks before him. He looked up, and his resemblance to Daniel striking yet fundamentally different. They same features arranged into a harder expression, same eyes without the warmth.

"That will be all, Rhodes," he said, waving dismissively.

The secretary bowed slightly and retreated, closing the door and leaving Sarah standing awkwardly in the center of the room.

"Sarah Dobbs." Bailey looked at her for a long while before he said. "Sit."

She perched on the edge of the indicated chair and folded her hands in her lap.

"Do you know why I've called you here?" Bailey asked, setting down his pen.

"No, sir."

"I have a proposition for you." He leaned back in his chair. "I find myself in need of additional household staff. A position has opened that might suit you."

Sarah stared at him, confused. "You want me to work in your house?"

"A personal assistant, of sorts." His eyes traveled over her in a way that made her skin crawl. "You'd have your own room, better food, and twice the wages you make at the mill."

"I don't understand. Why me? I have no training in household service."

Bailey's mouth curved into something not quite a smile. "Let's say I've heard promising things about your... abilities. You'd have special duties, reporting directly to me rather than the housekeeper."

The way he said "special duties" made Sarah's stomach turn. She'd heard stories about people who took "personal assistants" from among the prettier workers. It was merely a dignified version of going to Madame Abbess's house.

"I'm honored by the offer, sir," she said carefully. "But I'm content with my position at the mill."

Bailey's expression hardened. "Content? With the noise and filth? With half the pay and none of the comforts? I'm offering you an opportunity most mill girls would kill for."

"Perhaps they would, sir. But I know my work at the mill and I am good at it."

"This reluctance..." Bailey's eyes narrowed. "It wouldn't have anything to do with my son, would it?"

Sarah's heart skipped. "I don't understand, sir."

"Oh, I think you do." He stood, circling the desk to lean against it, until he was close for comfort. "You think I don't know about your little meetings at the library and Daniel's sudden interest in doing something about the working conditions?"

"Mr. Bailey and I have spoken only about books," Sarah said, fighting to keep her voice strong. "Nothing improper."

He laughed, a hollow sound. "Nothing improper. How quaint. Let me be perfectly clear, Miss Dobbs. My son may be going through a rebellious phase, but he is a Bailey. He has a future that doesn't include mill girls, no matter how pretty or literate they might be."

"I've never presumed otherwise, sir." Sarah's fingernails dug into her palms.

"Haven't you? Then why refuse my generous offer? What are you holding out for?" Bailey leaned closer. "Do you imagine my son will elevate you somehow and make you a lady? Trust me, girl, to Daniel, you're nothing but a curiosity and a temporary diversion."

"You don't know your son very well if you believe that," Sarah said before she could stop herself.

Bailey's eyes widened momentarily before

narrowing to dangerous slits. "And you think you know him better? How charmingly naive."

Sarah stood, no longer able to remain seated with him looming over her. "I have never wanted anything that wasn't mine to have, Mr. Bailey. I know my place in this world."

"Do you? Because from where I stand, you're forgetting it entirely." His voice dropped. "Pretty girls like you who step out of line don't last long in respectable employment. Madame Abbess is always looking for new faces at her establishment. Is that where you'd prefer to end up?"

The threat hung in the air, blatant and ugly. Sarah fought back the trembling in her legs.

"I would prefer to return to my work at the mill, sir," she said, her voice steadier than she felt. "I'm grateful for your consideration, but I must decline."

Bailey stared at her as if she'd suddenly spoken in a foreign language. Few people refused Edward Bailey anything, and certainly no mill girl had ever done so.

"You realize I could dismiss you immediately without reference."

"Yes, sir. But I haven't done anything to warrant dismissal, and the Northern Review seems quite interested in such practices lately." Sarah held his gaze, surprising even herself with her boldness.

"You're not as clever as you think you are, Miss Dobbs." He returned to his seat behind the desk. "You may return to the mill for now. But remember this conversation when winter comes and you're shivering in that drafty dormitory. Remember it when your fingers bleed from the burns of the rope and your lungs seize from cotton dust."

"I will, sir." Sarah moved toward the door, then paused. "And perhaps you might remember something too. Your son is a better man than you give him credit for."

Before he could respond, she let herself out, closing the door quietly behind her. She managed to maintain her composure through the grand hallway, past the curious stares of the kitchen staff, and beyond the back gates of the Bailey property.

Only when she reached the small copse of trees between the main house and the mill did her legs finally give way. Sarah sank onto the grass beneath an old oak, her whole body shaking as the reality of what had just happened and what she had just done washed over her.

Edward Bailey had all but propositioned her, threatened her, and she had refused him to his face.

She'd talked back to the most powerful man in Lancashire. Her job, her reputation, possibly her very safety now hung by the thinnest thread.

Sarah pressed her hands against her mouth to muffle the sobs that tore through her chest.

"Sarah? Good Lord, what's happened?"

She looked up to find Tommy Briggs standing a few feet away, his expression shifting from surprise to concern.

"Nothing. I'm fine." Sarah wiped hastily at her face. "Shouldn't you be at work?"

"The carding machine broke. We're idle until they fix it." Tommy crouched beside her. "You're clearly not fine. What's going on? Why aren't you at the knotter's room?"

"I had a meeting with Edward Bailey," she said in a rush. "He offered me a position in his household. As his 'personal assistant' with 'special duties.'"

Tommy's face darkened as he understood. "That old lecher. Did he touch you? If he laid a hand on you, I'll…"

"He didn't touch me." Sarah shook her head. "But his meaning was clear enough. And when I refused, he threatened me."

"The bastard," Tommy muttered. "What did he say?"

"I would be dismissed. And..." Sarah swallowed hard. "He mentioned me ending up at Madame Abbess's house."

Tommy sat heavily beside her, his youthful face tight with anger. "He can't send you to a bawdy house just for refusing him."

"He can do whatever he wants. He's Edward Bailey."

"The article in the Northern Review has him rattled," Tommy said. "That's why he's lashing out. But why target you specifically? Why not Annie or any other girl?"

Sarah hesitated. "He knows about Daniel and me."

"Daniel? You mean young Mr. Bailey?" Tommy's eyebrows shot up. "What about him?"

"We've been meeting at the library on Sundays." Saying it aloud made it sound both more and less significant than it felt.

"Huh?" Tommy's expression was skeptical.

Sarah wiped away the last of her tears. "We just talk, that's all."

"But you like him," Tommy said. It wasn't a question.

Sarah stared at her hands. "It doesn't matter if I do. His father made that perfectly clear."

"What did the old tyrant say?"

"I am nothing to him but a curiosity." The words still stung, and repeating did nothing to dull their edge. "He's right, of course. What else could I be?"

Tommy snorted. "Bailey's right about as often as a broken clock. Did you ever think maybe his son sees something in you that's worth seeing?"

"Don't be ridiculous. Daniel's world and mine don't intersect except by chance or charity."

"And yet you call him Daniel, not Mr. Bailey." Tommy nudged her shoulder gently. "Look, I'm not saying it's not complicated. God knows it is. But if there's one thing I've learned watching my aunt, it's that people aren't always bound by what's expected of them."

"Your aunt is a shopkeeper who bakes excellent pies. Hardly the same as crossing class lines that have existed for centuries."

"Says the mill girl who just told Edward Bailey where to stuff his indecent proposal." Tommy grinned. "Face it, Sarah. You've never been one to stay in your assigned place."

Sarah found herself smiling. "I can't believe I stood up to him. I've never been so frightened in my life."

"He's just a man. A rich, powerful, dangerous

man, but still just a man." Tommy plucked a blade of grass and twisted it between his fingers. "What are you going to do about his son?"

"Nothing. What can I do? His father is right about one thing, Daniel has a future that doesn't include me."

"Maybe. Or maybe something will change." Tommy looked toward the mill. "I mean things aren't the same as they were even a month ago."

"That doesn't change who Daniel is. Or who I am."

"No. But it might change what's possible." Tommy stood, offering her his hand. "Come on. Your tears have ruined half the grass. Mrs. Fletcher will wonder where you've gone."

Sarah accepted his help, brushing off her skirt. "Thank you. For listening."

"Anytime. That's what friends do." He studied her for a moment. "For what it's worth, I think young Bailey is lucky to have caught your interest, however brief or impossible it might be."

"It's worth more than you know," Sarah said quietly. "Now, tell me about this broken carding machine. Did you have anything to do with it?"

Tommy's innocent expression was so exaggerated that Sarah couldn't help laughing.

"Me? Sabotage a carding machine? I'm shocked you'd suggest such a thing." Tommy placed a hand over his heart in mock outrage. "Though if someone were to accidentally drop a metal buckle into the gears and then replace the guards so no one could see it until the machine was running at full speed... well, that would be quite clever, wouldn't it?"

Sarah shook her head, but her smile remained. "You're impossible."

"So I've been told. Usually right before I do something extremely possible that no one expected." He offered his arm in an exaggerated gentlemanly gesture. "Shall I escort you back to your place of employment, Miss Dobbs?"

"You shall, Mr. Briggs," Sarah replied, taking his arm. "Though if anyone asks, we never saw each other, and I certainly wasn't crying under a tree."

"Crying? You? I haven't the faintest idea what you're talking about." Tommy winked.

# CHAPTER 18

## Daniel

THE BREAKFAST ROOM was thick with silence, broken only by the clink of silverware against the fine china. Daniel pushed his eggs around his plate. He lost his appetite as he felt his father's gaze boring into him from across the table. Elizabeth Bailey kept her eyes on her teacup.

"Well?" Edward Bailey finally broke the silence. "I assume you've done the needful and prepared your statement for the Northern Review."

Daniel set down his fork. "I have not."

"I see." Edward's voice remained eerily calm. "Perhaps you misunderstood our conversation. This isn't a request. It's a requirement."

"I understood perfectly," Daniel replied, meeting his father's gaze. "I won't disavow the truth because every word in that article is accurate."

"Accuracy is irrelevant. Loyalty is what matters." Edward's knuckles whitened around his knife handle. "That article has already cost us a contract with the Whitby textile merchants. They don't want association with a mill described as 'barbaric' and 'inhumane.'"

"Perhaps they should reconsider their standards rather than their associations."

Edward's control slipped. "How dare you. After everything I've built for this family…"

"Built on what, Father? The broken backs of children and the desperation of families who can't survive on the wages you pay?" Daniel pushed his plate away. "I've seen the account books. The profits you're making could easily allow for better conditions."

"You understand nothing about business."

"I understand enough about humanity."

Elizabeth shifted uncomfortably. "Perhaps this conversation would be better continued privately…"

"No, Elizabeth," Edward cut her off. "Our son

believes himself the moral authority on mill management. Let him speak his piece at the family table." He turned to Daniel. "Go on, then. Tell us how you would run Bailey's Mill into the ground with your university ideals."

"I'd start by abolishing the fine system. It's theft, plain and simple." Daniel's voice strengthened. "Then raise wages to something people can actually live on. Improve safety measures and reduce shifts for children."

Edward laughed in mockery. "Brilliant. And watch as every other mill owner in Lancashire undercuts our prices and steals our contracts. We'd be bankrupt within a year."

"Not if we led by example. Not if we showed that treating workers like human beings actually improves productivity and quality."

"That's nothing but fantasy. The product of a mind that's never had to make difficult decisions." Edward wiped his mouth. "This is my final offer, Daniel. Get that wannabe to publish a retraction, apologize for your lapse in judgment, and all will be forgiven."

"And if I refuse?"

"Then you are barred from all mill operations, effective immediately. You will remain confined to the estate until you come to your senses." Edward's expression hardened. "No visits to town. No access to the mill grounds. No contact with that journalist or anyone associated with him."

Daniel stood, anger finally breaking through his restraint. "You can't confine me like a child. I'm twenty-two years old."

"You are living under my roof, eating my food, spending my money." Edward rose as well, his imposing figure rigid with fury. "Until you demonstrate the judgment and loyalty this family requires, you will abide by my rules."

"Your rules or your tyranny?" Daniel's hands shook slightly. "The article didn't make you look inhumane, Father. You managed that all on your own."

The sound of Edward's palm striking the table echoed through the room. Elizabeth flinched but remained silent.

"You ungrateful boy," Edward hissed. "Everything you have, came from the mill you're so eager to condemn."

"I'm well aware of where our money comes from," Daniel replied. "That's precisely why I can't stay silent anymore."

"Then consider yourself no longer part of this

business. The guards have been instructed to prevent your entry to the mill. Your allowance is suspended." Edward straightened his waistcoat. "When you're prepared to be reasonable, we can discuss your return to the family's good graces."

"And if that day never comes?"

Edward's gaze turned cold. "Then pray Catherine Harrington's family is willing to support a husband with neither inheritance nor prospects."

"Catherine deserves better than a marriage of convenience."

"What she deserves is immaterial. The engagement will proceed as planned." Edward moved toward the door. "You have until the announcement ball to reconsider your position. After that, certain decisions become irreversible."

Daniel sank back into his chair.

"He means it, you know," his mother said quietly. "Your father doesn't make idle threats."

"I know."

"And still you push him."

"What would you have me do, Mother? Pretend I don't see what's happening and ignore what we're doing to those people?"

Elizabeth sighed, reaching across the table to

touch his hand briefly. "I'm not criticizing your principles, Daniel. Just perhaps your tactics."

"You think I should apologize and take it all back?"

"I think there are ways to effect change that don't involve burning every bridge behind you." She studied him. "Though I suspect you're past hearing such counsel now."

Daniel ran a hand through his hair. "I can't retract the truth, Mother. I just can't."

"Then you'd better prepare for what comes next."

They lapsed into silence. After a moment, Daniel looked up at his mother with sudden clarity.

"You run a safe house," he said. "For girls who would have been sent to Madame Abbess's place and you help them find handy work."

Elizabeth's teacup clattered against its saucer. "Who told you that?"

"No one had to tell me. I've noticed things. Your mysterious errands and some household funds diverted to miscellaneous expenses."

"You always were too observant for your own good." Elizabeth's expression softened. "Yes. I help when I can."

"Why didn't you ever tell me?"

"Your father wouldn't approve. And I needed to

protect you from knowledge that might put you in a difficult position."

"I admire what you're doing," Daniel said earnestly. "But Mother, you deserve better too. The way he speaks to you, and dismisses you isn't right."

Elizabeth smiled sadly. "I made my choice long ago, Daniel. I've learned to find purpose within these confines." She hesitated. "But there's something you should know. Your father summoned Sarah Dobbs to the house yesterday."

Daniel stiffened. "Sarah? Why?"

"He offered her a position in the household. As his 'personal assistant.'" Elizabeth's emphasis conveyed everything the words didn't.

"He didn't."

"He did. And when she refused, he threatened her with dismissal and worse."

Daniel's hands clenched into fists. "How dare he. How dare he try to…"

"She stood up to him," Elizabeth interrupted, a hint of admiration in her voice. "She refused him outright and walked away with her dignity intact. I heard about it from the kitchen staff and they were quite impressed."

"Is she safe? Do you think he will retaliate?"

"For now, I think he's too shocked that a mill girl

refused him to do anything immediately." Elizabeth studied her son's face. "You care for her, don't you?"

Daniel didn't bother denying it. "I do. Though there seems to be an endless list of reasons why I shouldn't."

"The heart rarely consults reason before choosing its direction." Elizabeth's lips curved into a small smile. "She must be quite remarkable, this Sarah Dobbs."

"She is." Daniel found himself smiling despite everything. "She's intelligent, direct, uncompromising and she sees things as they are."

"Then she sounds exactly like someone you need in your life." Elizabeth reached for his hand again, and squeezed it gently. "Whatever path you choose, Daniel, you have my blessing."

"Even if that path leads me away from everything Father has planned?"

"Especially then." Elizabeth's eyes sparkled with unexpected mischief. "I married for family advantage and social position. Perhaps it's time a Bailey married for something better."

"Thank you, Mother." Daniel felt a weight lift, one he hadn't fully recognized until that moment. "Though I'm getting rather ahead of myself. Sarah has made it quite clear that any friendship between us is complicated enough without adding further entanglements."

"She's a sensible girl." Elizabeth nodded approvingly. "But sensible people have been known to change their minds when the right opportunity presents itself."

A knock at the door interrupted them. Arthur entered.

"Forgive the intrusion, but Miss Catherine Harrington has arrived for your promenade in the garden." His eyes conveyed silent sympathy. "She's waiting in the south parlor."

"Already? She wasn't expected until noon." Daniel groaned. "Please tell her I'll be there shortly."

As Arthur withdrew, Elizabeth laughed softly. "The trials of being a sought-after bachelor."

"This isn't helping matters, Mother." Daniel stood reluctantly. "Catherine will talk my ear off about wedding preparations I have no intention of participating in."

"Consider it practice." Elizabeth rose as well, smoothing her skirts. "A skill you'll need if you're planning to remake the Bailey family legacy."

"Diplomacy has never been my strong suit."

"Then perhaps it's time to develop new

strengths." She kissed his cheek lightly. "Good luck with Catherine."

Daniel watched his mother leave. How much else had he missed by accepting she was fragile at face value?

Catherine sat waiting in the south parlor, her blue dress arranged in perfect folds around her on the settee. A large portfolio rested on her lap, and several fabric samples lay spread on the table before her.

She brightened when Daniel entered. "There you are! I hope you don't mind my early arrival. I was simply too excited to wait."

"Of course not," Daniel lied smoothly. "Though I must admit, I'm not at my best this morning."

"Oh?" Catherine's brow furrowed delicately. "Nothing serious, I hope."

"Just a disagreement with my father."

"Ah." She waved dismissively. "Men's business. Well, I have something that will cheer you up immensely. Shall we walk in the garden? The weather is perfect for reviewing my ideas."

Daniel offered his arm, and they proceeded to the courtyard garden. Catherine immediately steered them towards a stone bench partially shaded by a flowering tree.

"Now then," she said, opening her portfolio with excitement. "I've selected several samples of lace for the wedding. The most exquisite piece comes from Jenkins Mill in Yorkshire." She extracted a delicate scrap of white lace. "Feel how fine it is. Almost like cobwebs."

Daniel touched the lace reluctantly. "It's very... intricate."

"They are produced by the most skilled child lacemakers in England," Catherine announced proudly. "Some as young as six, with the tiniest fingers you can imagine. Perfect for the finest details."

"Six?" Daniel frowned. "That seems extraordinarily young for such work."

"Oh, they start their training at four, but they don't produce export-quality work until six or seven," Catherine continued, oblivious to his discomfort. "The Jenkins family says the children's eyesight is sharpest before ten, so they get the best work in those early years."

"And what happens to them after ten?"

Catherine looked up, puzzled by his tone. "I suppose they move on to other tasks. I haven't inquired into those details."

"Perhaps you should." Daniel couldn't keep the

edge from his voice. "Before purchasing products made by children who will likely be blind by fifteen."

"Daniel," Catherine laughed lightly, "you're being adorably naïve. This is how fine lace has always been made. Would you have us return to the dark ages of inferior products simply because modern sensibilities have grown soft?"

"I'd have us consider the human cost of our luxuries."

"The humans in question are being paid for their work," Catherine pointed out. "Many would have no income otherwise. Really, it's a kindness to provide them employment."

Daniel stared at her, truly seeing her for perhaps the first time. "A kindness. To put a four-year-old to work on delicate stitching that will ruin their eyesight?"

"You're exaggerating the hardship." Catherine patted his hand as if soothing a child. "These notions of yours are charming in their way, but you'll outgrow them after we're married. My father says all young men go through a phase of impractical idealism."

"This isn't a phase, Catherine." Daniel moved the lace samples aside. "It's a fundamental difference in how we see the world."

"What an odd thing to say." She tilted her head, studying him. "We see the world exactly as we were raised to see it, as people of our class and standing. The occasional youthful rebellion against convention is to be expected, but it passes."

"And if it doesn't?"

"It always does." Catherine's certainty was absolute. "Once you have the responsibilities of a husband and future mill owner, these flights of fancy will naturally give way to practical considerations."

"What if I don't want them to?"

Catherine laughed again. "You speak as if you have a choice in the matter. Society functions because we all eventually accept our proper roles." She reached for his hand. "Now, about the wedding breakfast. I've been considering a French-inspired menu..."

"Catherine..."

"Yes?"

"This marriage cannot happen..."

# CHAPTER 19

*Sarah*

Sarah traced her fingertip over the worn leather spine of "A Tale of Two Cities." The small library sat empty except for her. Her legs ached from standing all day at the bench, yet she'd walked straight here after her shift instead of heading to dinner.

Three days since she'd seen Daniel. Three days since their last conversation, when she'd pulled away from whatever was brewing between them. Was she too harsh, too quick to build a wall between them? The questions nagged her like a loose thread she couldn't stop tugging.

The door creaked open behind her. Sarah turned, expecting and hoping to see Daniel. Instead, Arthur Evans stepped inside, his posture impeccable as always. He carried a parcel wrapped in brown paper.

"Miss Dobbs." He inclined his head slightly. "I hope I'm not disturbing you."

"Not at all, Mr. Evans." Sarah straightened, suddenly conscious.

"Mr. Bailey asked me to deliver this." He held out the package. "He regrets he cannot bring it himself."

Sarah accepted it. "Thank you."

Arthur lingered for a moment, as if wanting to say more, then simply nodded. "Good evening, Miss Dobbs."

He left as quietly as he'd arrived, the door closing with a soft click behind him.

Sarah waited until his footsteps faded before unwrapping the parcel. Inside was a leather-bound copy of "Great Expectations" and a folded letter. Her heart jumped.

She broke the seal and unfolded the paper.

*Dear Sarah,*

*I hope this finds you well. I've been confined to the estate by my father. It is the price of my involvement with the Northern Review article. No mill visits, no town excursions, and most disappointingly, no Sunday meet-*

*ings at our library. (Yes, I've come to think of it as "ours," presumptuous as that may be.)*

*First and most importantly, my mother told me about my father's summons and his inappropriate "offer" to you. I'm mortified and furious on your behalf. Please know I had no knowledge of his intentions, though that hardly excuses what happened. Your courage in standing up to him is remarkable, if unsurprising to me.*

*As for my situation, it's grown rather medieval. Father has suspended my allowance and barred me from mill operations.*

*I've included "Great Expectations" because Pip's journey from ignorance to understanding mirrors my own in many ways. Though I daresay you'd make a far more compelling Estella than the original.*

*I miss our conversations. The library is a poorer place without you in it.*

*Yours,*

*Daniel*

Sarah turned the letter over and noticed tiny words squeezed into the bottom margin:

*P.S. I hope one day, you can accept my offer of friendship.*

Heat rushed to her face. She ran her fingers over the words as if they might dissolve under her touch.

"Such a ridiculous man," she murmured, but couldn't stop the smile spreading across her face.

She tucked the letter into her pocket and wrapped the book in the brown paper. Reluctantly, she left the library's sanctuary and stepped into the cool evening air.

"There you are!"

Tommy leaned against the mill yard wall, pushing himself upright when he spotted her. Sarah stopped short at the sight of him. His left eye was swollen nearly shut, a purple bruise blooming across his cheekbone.

"Good Lord, what happened to your face?" Sarah rushed forward.

"I walked into a door." Tommy grinned, then winced at the movement. "A door shaped like Bailey's new security men."

"Oh my God!" Sarah looked around nervously. "Are you okay?."

Tommy fell into step beside her as they headed toward the mill gates. "Though I'd rather not meet any more of Bailey's hired help today."

"When did this happen?"

"This morning. Two men caught me handing out petition sheets near the weaving shed." Tommy touched his bruised eye gingerly. "Said they were 'delivering a message from management about appropriate workplace behavior.'"

Sarah's stomach turned. "They could have killed you."

"Nah, they were careful. It was bruises only, so nothing's broken. They can't have workers thinking they're being murdered for speaking up." Tommy's light tone didn't match the hardness in his good eye. "Besides, we got fifteen more signatures before they showed up."

"Is it worth it?" She gestured at his face.

"Someone's got to stand up, Sarah." Tommy shrugged. "Might as well be me. My pretty face was overrated anyway."

Sarah shook her head. "You're impossible."

"So you keep saying. Yet here I am. Would you like to go to my aunt's for dinner?" Tommy offered his arm with exaggerated gallantry. "Unless you'd rather not?"

"Of course not. I'm starving." Sarah took his arm. "Does Mrs. Winters know you've been picking fights with Bailey's men?"

"It wasn't exactly my choice of dance partners," Tommy protested. "And no, she doesn't know. So keep your mouth shut about it, will you? She'll only worry."

Mrs. Winters' small house sat behind her bakery shop, a warm light glowing in the windows. Tommy rapped on the door, and Sarah's heart jumped when it swung open to reveal Annie standing in the doorway.

"Sarah!" Annie flung her arms around her friend. "I wasn't sure you'd come!"

Sarah hugged her back fiercely. "I've missed you so much."

"Me too. It's been impossible without you." Annie pulled back to look at her. "You look tired. Are they working you too hard? Is that awful Hawk still..." She stopped suddenly, noticing Tommy. Her expression cooled. "Oh. Hello."

"Hello, Annie." Tommy shifted uncomfortably. "You look well."

Annie's eyes widened as she took in his bruised face. "What happened to you?"

"Nothing important." Tommy tried to smile but grimaced instead.

Annie looked like she wanted to say more but pressed her lips together and stepped back. "Come in. Mrs. Winters has dinner ready."

The small kitchen smelled wonderfully of roasted meat and baking bread. Mrs. Winters stood at the stove, her gray hair escaping its pins in all directions.

"There you are my dears! Right on time!" She turned, then gasped. "Thomas Briggs! What in heaven's name happened to your face?"

"I fell," Tommy said quickly.

"Into someone's fist, by the look of it." Mrs. Winters planted her hands on her hips. "Who was it? Those Clayton boys again?"

"It doesn't matter, Aunt Bess." Tommy glanced at Annie, who studiously avoided his gaze. "I'm fine."

"Sit down, all of you." Mrs. Winters waved them to the table. "Annie's made the most wonderful apple tarts for dessert. The girl's a natural baker."

Annie blushed. "They're nothing special."

"Nonsense!" Mrs. Winters began serving stew. "She's been a godsend these past weeks. I've even taught her to manage the money box."

"That's wonderful," Sarah said, genuinely pleased. "You've found your feet quickly."

"I've been lucky," Annie said softly. "Not everyone has somewhere to go when they're dismissed."

Her eyes flickered to Tommy's bruised face. She was clearly worried.

Tommy noticed. "It looks worse than it is."

"I didn't ask," Annie replied stiffly.

Sarah kicked Tommy's foot under the table. He cleared his throat.

"Annie," he began, "I know you don't want to hear it, but I'm sorry. About everything. You were right, and I was wrong, and I've regretted it every day since you left."

Annie continued eating her stew, not looking up.

"Your pamphlet cost me my job, and my home ," she said quietly.

"I know." Tommy pushed his bowl away. "And I'd give anything to take it back. I was stupid and reckless, and I put you in danger without thinking."

"Yes, you did."

"I miss you," Tommy said simply. "Not just as... whatever we might have been. But as my friend. The one person who saw past all my nonsense."

Annie looked up. "You have plenty of nonsense to see past."

"More every day," Tommy agreed. "And no one to tell me when I'm being an idiot."

"You never listened anyway."

"I'm listening now." Tommy leaned forward. "I'm listening, and I'm asking for another chance. Not for anything but to be in your life again, on your terms."

Annie studied him, taking in his bruised face and

pleading expression. "You're still involved in all of it, aren't you?. Nothing's changed."

"Some things have." Tommy glanced at Sarah. "I'm trying to be smarter about it and to be more careful."

"Is that what you call this?" Annie gestured to his face.

"This is a temporary setback in my new careful approach to social change," Tommy offered a cautious smile.

Annie's lips twitched. "You're impossible."

"So I'm told." Tommy's smile widened. "Frequently."

"Stop smiling. It doesn't help your case." But Annie's severe expression had softened. "Your eye needs a cold compress. It's swelling worse by the minute."

"Does this mean you forgive me?" Tommy asked hopefully.

"It means your face is a disaster and I can't stand looking at it without doing something." Annie stood and went to the cupboard, pulling out a clean cloth. "Mrs. Winters, do you have any ice?"

"In the shop cold box, dear." Mrs. Winters winked at Sarah as Annie left the room. "Young love. So dramatic."

"We're not..." Tommy started.

"Oh, hush." Mrs. Winters waved him off. "Now, Sarah, tell me how you've been. Any news?"

Sarah thought of Daniel's letter in her pocket. "Nothing exciting."

"Really? Because I heard young Mr. Bailey has been banned from the mill by his father." Mrs. Winters raised an eyebrow.

"How do you know that?" Sarah asked, surprised.

"Their housekeeper's cousin works in our local pub." Mrs. Winters ladled more stew into Sarah's bowl. "Apparently there was quite the row. The old man's furious that his son spoke to that journalist."

Annie returned with a cloth-wrapped bundle of ice. "Here." She pressed it gently to Tommy's eye. He winced but didn't pull away.

"Thank you," he said softly.

Annie nodded, letting her hand linger a moment before sitting down again, closer to Tommy than before.

"But that's not even the most interesting part," Mrs. Winters continued. "They say old Bailey's pushing ahead with the Harrington engagement. He announced the wedding date to half the county's elite at the Marshalls' dinner party last night."

Sarah's spoon clattered against her bowl. "What?"

"Oh yes. It's a June wedding, apparently. All very rushed, but the old man's determined." Mrs. Winters didn't seem to notice Sarah's reaction. "Can't say I blame the girl for snatching him up. He's handsome, educated, and the heir to the biggest mill in Lancashire. That Catherine Harrington always did have an eye for advantage."

"The wedding is... definite, then?" Sarah asked, fighting to keep her voice casual.

"According to Mrs. Thompson, who heard it from Mrs. Bailey's lady's maid herself, the announcement will be in the papers by week's end." Mrs. Winters leaned forward. "Though some say the young man doesn't seem particularly enthusiastic about his good fortune."

Sarah felt three pairs of eyes on her. She focused on her stew, suddenly not hungry at all.

"That's hardly surprising," Tommy said. "From what I've heard, young Bailey doesn't agree with his father on much these days."

"Well, agreement rarely factors into these arrangements." Mrs. Winters shrugged. "Money marries money, business marries connections. The way of the world."

"Not always," Annie said quietly. "Some people choose differently."

"True enough," Mrs. Winters agreed. "Though it takes a particular kind of courage to defy expectations." She glanced meaningfully at Sarah. "More stew, dear?"

"No, thank you." Sarah managed a smile. "But I'd love to try Annie's apple tarts."

The conversation mercifully turned to Annie's new baking skills and Mrs. Winters' plans to expand her shop offerings. Sarah participated enough to avoid suspicion, but Daniel's letter seemed to burn against her side, the words now took on a bittersweet edge.

Engaged to be married. Of course he was. What else had she expected?

Later, as they prepared to leave, Annie pulled Sarah aside.

"You've been quiet all night," she said. "Is everything all right?"

"Just tired," Sarah lied. "The work has been busy."

Annie studied her face. "It's not just that, though, is it?"

Sarah hesitated. "I received a letter today."

"From?"

"Daniel Bailey."

Annie's eyes widened. "The mill owner's son?

Why would he…" Understanding dawned across her face. "Oh, Sarah."

"It's nothing," Sarah said quickly. "We've talked a few times. That's all."

"That's all?" Annie didn't look convinced. "And the news about his engagement bothers you because…?"

"It doesn't," Sarah insisted. "It's exactly what should happen. What always happens."

Annie squeezed her hand. "Sarah Dobbs, you've never been a good liar."

"There's nothing to lie about. He's Daniel Bailey, heir to the mill and I'm a knotter with callused hands and no prospects."

"And yet he writes you letters."

Sarah had no answer for that.

"Be careful," Annie said softly. "Men like him live in a different world."

"I know that" Sarah said. "Better than anyone."

## CHAPTER 20

*Daniel*

Daniel had been up for hours, reading reports throughout Lancashire that he'd had Arthur smuggle in. His confinement had turned his bedroom into both sanctuary and prison but it was a space where he could think freely but could not act on those thoughts.

A soft knock at the door interrupted his reading.

. . .

"Come in," Daniel called, hastily covering the reports with blank paper.

Arthur entered, carrying a silver tray with coffee and the morning newspaper. "Breakfast, sir. And today's paper."

"Thank you, Arthur." Daniel accepted the coffee gratefully. "Anything interesting in the news?"

Arthur hesitated. "Perhaps you should see for yourself, sir."

Something in his tone made Daniel reach for the newspaper immediately. He unfolded it and froze. There, on the society page, was the announcement:

*ENGAGEMENT ANNOUNCED*

*Mr. Edward Bailey and Mr. Richard Harrington are pleased to announce the engagement of their children, Mr. Daniel Bailey and Miss Catherine Harrington. The wedding is to take place in June at St. Paul's Cathedral. The union joins two of Lancashire's most prominent families...*

The cup in Daniel's hand clattered against its saucer. "He actually did it."

"I'm sorry, sir." Arthur stood uncomfortably by the door. "The announcement appeared in both the local paper and the London Times this morning."

Daniel stared at the words, printed in neat black ink for all of Lancashire to see. His life, decided and announced without his consent.

"Where is my father now?"

"In his study, sir. He's meeting with Mr. Harrington at noon to discuss the wedding arrangements."

. . .

Daniel stood, crumpling the newspaper in his fist. "Please inform my father I wish to speak with him immediately."

"Sir, perhaps when you're calmer…"

"Now, Arthur." Daniel's voice left no room for argument. "Please."

Arthur nodded and left. Daniel paced the room, the crumpled newspaper still clutched in his hand. By the time Arthur returned, he'd worked himself into a cold fury.

"Your father will see you in his study," Arthur reported. "He says you have ten minutes before Mr. Thorne arrives for their meeting."

"How generous of him." Daniel straightened his collar and headed for the door.

. . .

"Sir?" Arthur called after him. "Perhaps a diplomatic approach would be…"

"I'm past diplomacy, Arthur."

Daniel strode through the manor's polished hallways, nodding curtly to servants who quickly looked away. They'd all seen the announcement, of course. Everyone had.

He didn't bother knocking on his father's study door.

Edward Bailey looked up from his desk, unsurprised. "Ah, Daniel. I take it you've seen the papers."

Daniel tossed the crumpled newspaper onto his father's immaculate desk. "You announced my engagement without my consent."

. . .

"Did I need it?" Edward leaned back in his chair, studying his son. "The arrangements have been in place for years. The Harringtons are eager to proceed. Catherine is a suitable match in every way."

"Except for the minor detail that I refuse to marry her."

"Refuse?" Edward laughed. "On what grounds? That she's beautiful, wealthy, and from a good family? That she adores you despite your recent... eccentricities?"

"On the grounds that I don't love her and never will." Daniel planted his hands on the desk, leaning forward. "I won't do it, Father. Announce what you like, but I won't stand in that church."

Edward's amusement vanished. "You will do as you're told."

. . .

"I'm not a child anymore."

"No, you're my son and heir to everything I've built." Edward stood, matching Daniel's stance. "And you will fulfill your obligations to this family."

"Or what? You'll disinherit me? We've been through this already."

"This isn't just about your inheritance, Daniel." Edward's voice dropped, becoming dangerously quiet. "This is about that mill girl."

Daniel froze. "What?"

"Sarah Dobbs." Edward smiled thinly. "Did you think I wouldn't find out about your little library meetings? Your letters? Arthur is loyal, but my house has many eyes and ears."

. . .

"Leave her out of this." Daniel straightened. "She has nothing to do with my decision."

"Doesn't she? You started questioning everything about the mill after meeting her. Now you're rejecting a match that any rational man would grab with both hands." Edward circled the desk, eyes never leaving his son's face. "You fancy yourself in love with a knotter."

"My feelings for Sarah are none of your concern."

"So, there are feelings." Edward nodded as if confirming a suspicion. "I suspected as much when she refused my offer of employment."

"Your 'offer' was an insult," Daniel snapped, his temper flaring. "Did you really think she would accept becoming your mistress?"

. . .

"I thought she'd recognize an opportunity to improve her station." Edward shrugged. "Most mill girls would. They're practical about survival, if nothing else."

"She has more dignity and courage than you could possibly understand."

"How charming." Edward's expression hardened. "Let me be perfectly clear, Daniel. I will not allow my son and heir to throw away his future on some workhouse orphan who tied knots for a living."

"Allow?" Daniel laughed bitterly. "You can't control who I love."

"Love?" Edward scoffed. "Is that what you're calling it? This fascination with a pretty face from the factory floor?"

"You know nothing about her."

. . .

"I know everything about her." Edward returned to his desk, pulling out a thin file. "Sarah Dobbs. Born 1860. Orphaned at seven when her parents died of fever. Raised at St. Michael's Workhouse until age eighteen, when she was apprenticed to our mill. Currently employed as a knotter for one year, four months." He closed the file. "Unremarkable in every way, except for basic literacy and the apparent ability to charm my foolish son."

Daniel's hands clenched into fists. "Are you finished?"

"Not quite." Edward leaned forward. "This girl has no references beyond Bailey's Mill, no family connections, no prospects. If I dismiss her, no decent mill in Lancashire would hire her. If I spread the word that she's a troublemaker or a thief, she'd be unemployable entirely."

. . .

"You wouldn't," Daniel said, but uncertainty crept into his voice.

"To protect the Bailey name and legacy? I most certainly would." Edward's voice was matter of fact. "Her options would become extremely limited. Perhaps Madame Abbess would take her in."

"You'd destroy an innocent woman's life to control me?" Daniel stared at his father, truly seeing him perhaps for the first time. "What kind of man does that make you?"

"A father. A father protecting his son from a disastrous mistake." Edward spread his hands. "The choice is simple, Daniel. Marry Catherine Harrington as arranged, or watch your mill girl lose everything."

"This is blackmail."

. . .

"This is business." Edward checked his pocket watch. "Thorne will be here any minute. I suggest you take the day to consider your position carefully. The Harringtons are hosting a dinner party on Friday to celebrate the engagement. You will attend, smiling appropriately, with your future bride on your arm."

"And if I refuse?"

"Then Miss Dobbs will be dismissed by week's end, with a reference that ensures she never works in decent employment again." Edward's eyes were cold. "I'd hate to see such a promising young woman reduced to... less savory occupations."

Daniel felt physically ill. "You'd really do that to her."

"Without hesitation." Edward straightened his cuffs. "The wedding will proceed, Daniel. Whether you come to your senses or I force your hand, the outcome will be the same. The only question is how many lives you destroy with your stubbornness."

A knock at the door signaled Thorne's arrival.

"We're finished here," Edward said dismissively. "I expect your decision by tomorrow morning, though I hardly think there's a decision to make. Even you aren't selfish enough to sacrifice that girl's future for your own romantic notions."

Daniel wanted to argue, to rage, to overturn the desk and every perfectly arranged item on it. Instead, he turned and walked out, brushing past Thorne without a word.

He stalked through the house, not stopping until he reached his rooms and slammed the door behind him.

. . .

Arthur looked up from where he was arranging Daniel's freshly laundered shirts. One look at Daniel's face and he set down his work.

"It didn't go well, I take it."

"He's announced the engagement to the entire country." Daniel paced the room like a caged animal. "And now he's threatening to destroy Sarah if I don't comply."

Arthur's carefully neutral expression slipped. "Miss Dobbs? How would he…"

"He would dismiss her without reference. Blacklist her from every respectable business in Lancashire." Daniel ran his hands through his hair. "You know what happens to mill girls with no references and no family."

"They go to Madame Abbess," Arthur said quietly.

. . .

"Exactly." Daniel stopped pacing, sinking into a chair. "He knows about our meetings."

"I'm sorry, sir. I tried to be discreet."

"It's not your fault. My father has spies everywhere." Daniel stared at his hands. "What am I supposed to do now? If I refuse to marry Catherine, Sarah pays the price. If I comply, I lose..." He trailed off, unable to finish the thought.

"You lose the chance to choose your own path," Arthur finished for him. "And possibly the woman you love."

Daniel looked up sharply. "I never said I loved her."

. . .

"With respect, sir, you didn't need to." Arthur began straightening items on Daniel's desk, giving him a moment to collect himself. "Perhaps Miss Dobbs could seek employment outside Lancashire? Beyond your father's influence?"

"With what resources? On what references? She has nothing and no one." Daniel stood again, unable to sit still. "This is exactly how he controls everyone. He finds their vulnerabilities and exploits them without mercy."

"What will you do, sir?"

"I don't know." Daniel moved to the window, staring out at the mill in the distance. "My father has spent his life turning people into pawns in his games. I refused to be one, so now he's using Sarah instead."

"Perhaps you should warn Miss Dobbs and explain the situation."

. . .

"And tell her what? That my father will destroy her life unless I marry a woman I don't love?" Daniel shook his head. "She'd blame herself. Or worse, she'd try to remove herself from the equation to protect me."

"She does seem to have a strong sense of self-sacrifice," Arthur agreed. "Though perhaps you underestimate her resilience."

Daniel turned back to the room. "I should write to her. At least to explain about the engagement announcement before she hears about it elsewhere."

"I believe that ship has sailed, sir. The papers have been circulating since early morning."

Daniel closed his eyes briefly. "She'll think I lied to her."

. . .

"Not if you explain." Arthur retrieved writing paper and a pen from the desk. "Shall I deliver a letter to the usual place?"

"Yes. Thank you." Daniel sat at the desk, staring at the blank paper. How could he possibly explain this situation? *Dear Sarah, Please ignore the announcement of my engagement. My father is blackmailing me with your future...*

"Sir?" Arthur interrupted his thoughts. "If I might make an observation?"

"Please do. I'm clearly in need of wiser counsel than my own at the moment."

"In my experience, the truth, however complicated or unpleasant, is usually preferable to even the most well-intentioned deception." Arthur placed the pen beside the paper. "Miss Dobbs strikes me as someone who values honesty."

. . .

Daniel nodded slowly. "You're right, of course."

He began to write, crossing out and restarting several times before producing a letter he found acceptable. He sealed it carefully and handed it to Arthur.

"Will you make sure she gets this? It's important that she understands."

"I'll see to it personally." Arthur tucked the letter into his pocket. "And sir? If I may be so bold... your father underestimates you. Perhaps that gives you an advantage he doesn't anticipate."

Daniel gave him a tired smile. "I hope you're right, Arthur. Because right now, I can't see a way out of this that doesn't end badly for someone I care about."

CHAPTER 21

*S*arah

"Pass the wax, would you?" Mrs. Fletcher waved her gnarled hand toward Sarah without looking up from her work.

Sarah slid the small tin across the workbench, careful not to disturb the intricate rope patterns laid out between them.

"Did you see the papers?" Bessie Wright whispered from the next table. "Young Mr. Bailey's engagement is official."

"To that Harrington girl," Jane Morris nodded. "It's a June wedding, they say. It must be very fancy."

Sarah kept her head down, pretending not to hear as she worked another complex sailor's knot into the replacement belt for the carding machine. The newspapers had been plastered with the announcement for days, making her stomach twist each time she caught sight of it.

The door banged open and Mr. Thorne strode in, followed by two men in expensive suits whom Sarah had never seen before. The room fell silent as every woman straightened at her station.

"Continue working," Thorne snapped, then turned to his companions. "As you can see, gentlemen, our knotter's room operates with traditional methods. Two workers per station, one belt repair at a time."

The taller visitor made a note in a small book. "That's inefficient. Marshall's Mill has implemented a stretching system. Four stations per worker and it doubles the output."

"Indeed," Thorne agreed. "Which is precisely what I've been instructed to implement here, effective immediately."

Mrs. Fletcher's head shot up. "What was that, Mr. Thorne?"

Thorne faced the room, his thin lips stretched into what might have been a smile on a warmer face.

"By order of Mr. Bailey, beginning today, each worker will manage four stations instead of two. The gentlemen from the council assure me this is standard practice at modern mills."

A murmur of disbelief circulated through the room.

"Four stations?" Mary Cooper shook her head. "We can barely manage two properly."

"Your opinion wasn't requested, Cooper," Thorne said. "This decision comes directly from management."

Sarah set down her work. "The knots won't hold if we rush them and once the knots are weak, it means the belts will break."

"Then don't rush, Dobbs. Work faster." Thorne turned to his visitors. "As you can see, there's some resistance to improvement. Always is with the older workers."

"I've been here one year," Sarah pointed out. "Hardly an 'older worker.' And it's about our safety."

The shorter visitor glanced at her with mild interest. "The girl has a point about quality control."

"Quality will be maintained through random inspections," Thorne said. "Now, I'll need half of you to relocate to stations on the west wall. Fletcher, reorganize your team."

Mrs. Fletcher stepped forward, wiping her hands on her apron. "Mr. Thorne, if we double the workload, we need more time per belt. These aren't simple repairs. One mistake and a belt snaps at full speed."

"The timeline remains the same. Ten belts per worker per day, now from four stations instead of two." Thorne consulted his pocket watch. "You have ten minutes to reorganize. I expect everything to be in full production when I return."

He turned to leave with the visitors following in his wake.

"This is madness," Mrs. Fletcher muttered once they were gone. "Four stations? We'll be running all day."

"It's not possible," Sarah agreed, looking around at the stunned faces of her coworkers. "Someone will get hurt."

"Someone always does," Mrs. Fletcher sighed. "But that's not the management's concern, is it? Come on, girls. We haven't got much choice."

They shuffled reluctantly to their new positions. Sarah found herself at the far end of the room, responsible for four workbenches spread too far apart for comfort. She'd need to dash between them constantly to keep pace.

Within an hour, the strain became evident. Women rushed from station to station, abandoning half-finished work to check on other belts.

Sarah wiped sweat from her brow as she raced to her third station, where a heavy drive belt needed a reinforced splice. Her shoulders ached from the constant turning, and her back protested the awkward positions required to reach across the wider workbenches.

A sharp cry from the opposite wall made her look up. Lily Banks, the youngest knotter at barely fifteen, had slumped against her workbench, her face pale with exhaustion.

"Lily?" Sarah called. "Are you all right?"

The girl nodded weakly. "Just dizzy. I haven't eaten since yesterday."

"Take a moment," Mrs. Fletcher advised. "Sit down before you fall."

"I can't," Lily gestured to her unfinished work. "Thorne will dock my pay."

She pushed herself upright and stumbled toward the big repair loom where a massive belt hung suspended. As she reached for her tools, her foot slipped on a scrap of leather.

What happened next seemed to unfold in terrible slow motion. Lily's hand shot out to catch herself, plunging directly into the partially disassembled gear mechanism of the repair loom. The metal teeth designed to grip leather seized her flesh instead. Her scream pierced the air as the machine caught two fingers and dragged them into its workings.

The women rushed forward and Sarah reached Lily first, slamming the emergency stop lever with all her strength. The machine ground to a halt, but Lily's hand remained trapped, blood already pooling on the floor below.

"Get Thorne!" Mrs. Fletcher shouted. "And someone fetch water!"

Sarah examined the machine, looking for a way to release the girl without causing more damage. Lily sobbed, her face drained of color.

"Hold still," Sarah told her. "We'll get you out."

She grabbed a pry bar from the tool rack and wedged it between the gears, creating just enough space for Mrs. Fletcher to slide Lily's mangled hand free. The damage was horrific. Two of her fingers were crushed beyond recognition, and the third was barely hanging on.

Thorne burst into the room, took one glance at the bloody scene, and barked, "Get her away from the machine. Clean that up before it stains the belt."

"She needs a doctor," Sarah said, helping Lily to a

bench while Mrs. Fletcher wrapped the girl's hand in a clean cloth that immediately soaked red. "Now, Mr. Thorne."

"The mill doctor checks injuries at four o'clock," Thorne replied. "She can wait in the infirmary."

"Wait?" Sarah stared at him in disbelief. "She could bleed to death by four!"

Lily swayed, her eyes rolling back as she slumped against Sarah's shoulder.

"She's just fainted," Thorne said dismissively. "Wrap it tighter and get back to work. We're behind schedule as it is."

Sarah stood, her bloodstained hands clenched at her sides. "No."

The room went deadly quiet.

"What did you say, Dobbs?" Thorne's voice dropped dangerously.

"I said no. We're not working until Lily sees a doctor." Sarah looked around at the pale faces of her coworkers. "This happened because we're being forced to work beyond human capacity."

Mrs. Fletcher stepped to her side. "She's right, Mr. Thorne. The girl needs a doctor."

One by one, the other women set down their tools.

Thorne's face flushed purple. "This is insubordination! I'll have all of you dismissed!"

"Dismiss us, then," Sarah replied, surprising herself. "But explain to Mr. Bailey why his entire knotter's room walked out at once. Explain why production did not meet the day's quota."

The women around her nodded.

Thorne glared at Sarah. "You think you're clever, Dobbs. You think because young Mr. Bailey took an interest in you, you're untouchable."

Sarah felt her face grow hot as whispers rippled through the room.

"This isn't about me," she said firmly. "Lily needs a doctor."

"Fine," Thorne spat. "Fletcher, take the girl to Dr. Morris in town. The rest of you, back to work."

"Not until she's seen to properly," Sarah insisted.

Thorne's thin lips pressed into a bloodless line. "You're dismissed, Dobbs. No pay for today or tomorrow. Consider yourself fortunate I don't make it permanent."

"But…"

"Get out before I change my mind," Thorne hissed. "And the rest of you… anyone not at their station in one minute will join her."

The women hesitated, looking between Sarah and Thorne.

"It's all right," Sarah told them. "Go back to work. Make sure Lily's taken care of."

Mrs. Fletcher squeezed her arm. "We'll see to her."

Sarah gathered her few belongings, acutely aware of Thorne's eyes boring into her back. She left the knotter's room with her head high, though her hands trembled.

Outside, the mill yard stretched emptier than she'd ever seen it during working hours. With no pay for two days, she'd barely be able to afford bread, let alone her portion of coal for the dormitory stove. But she couldn't regret standing up for Lily. Some things mattered more than money.

Without consciously deciding, Sarah found herself walking toward the small library. She hadn't been back since learning of Daniel's engagement, but something pulled her there now. A need for peace, perhaps, or the comfort of books that asked nothing of her.

The library door stood slightly ajar. Sarah hesitated, then pushed it open. Sunlight streamed through the dusty windows, illuminating the empty room. No Daniel today, of course. He was probably busy with wedding preparations and selecting china patterns with Catherine Harrington.

The thought stung more than it should have.

Sarah moved to the window seat where they'd exchanged books and letters. A fresh volume waited there, bound in green leather with gold lettering: "Pride and Prejudice" by Jane Austen. Beside it lay a sealed envelope with her name written in Daniel's handwriting.

She picked up the letter, weighing it in her palm. Why was she doing this to herself? He was engaged to another woman. Whatever had passed between them could never be anything real. She'd been foolish to imagine otherwise.

Still, her fingers broke the seal before she could reconsider.

The letter inside was short, the handwriting less careful than usual, as if written in haste:

*Miss Dobbs,*

*You have no doubt seen the announcement of my engagement to Miss Catherine Harrington in the papers. I felt it necessary to clarify certain matters between us before rumors might spread.*

*Our occasional conversations about books were a pleasant diversion, however, I fear you may have misin-*

*terpreted my attention as something more significant. This was never my intention.*

*A man in my position must maintain certain standards, and while I found your literacy unusual for someone of your background, we both know such differences in station cannot be overcome. I am to marry a woman of breeding and education, as has always been intended.*

*I must insist that our meetings end immediately. It would be inappropriate for me to continue any association that might cause gossip or distress to my future wife. I trust you understand that what might have seemed like friendship to you was merely a momentary curiosity on my part.*

*Do not attempt to contact me again. The books were my father's property, and I should not have allowed them to circulate among the workers. Please return any still in your possession to the library.*

*Daniel Bailey*

Sarah read the letter twice. The formality of "Daniel Bailey" after weeks of "Yours, Daniel" struck her like a physical blow.

*You come from different world than mine, and we both know such differences cannot be bridged.*

Of course they couldn't. She'd known that from the beginning, hadn't she? Their conversations had been nothing but a temporary distraction for him, a curious diversion from the boredom of his privileged life.

Sarah's eyes burned. She would not cry. Not here, not over this. She'd survived the workhouse, survived Bailey's Mill, survived Edward Bailey's insulting "offer." She would survive Daniel's dismissal too.

But the tears came anyway, hot and unwelcome. She sank onto the window seat, the letter clutched in her trembling hands and let them fall. Just for a moment, just in this empty room where no one could see, she allowed herself to mourn the foolish dreams she'd never admitted to having.

He was just like his father after all. Different methods, perhaps, but the same assumption that people like her were disposable, and their feelings inconsequential.

"Stupid," she whispered to herself. "So stupid."

## CHAPTER 22

*S*arah

SARAH DRAGGED her boot against the cobblestones as she made her way back to the dormitory. Daniel's letter was still pressed against her side where she'd tucked it into her pocket, and each step made the paper crinkle like it was mocking her. She still has to worry about no pay for 2 days.

A crowd was gathered outside the mill gates. Sarah frowned and quickened her pace. As she drew closer, she spotted Tommy standing on an overturned crate, gesturing passionately while speaking to about twenty workers clustered around him.

"They want us broken!" Tommy shouted, his voice carrying across the yard. "They'd rather see us starved than united!"

Sarah pushed through to the front, catching Tommy's eye. He nodded slightly before continuing.

"Bailey cuts our wages, then implements a stretching system that forces us to do twice the work. And when we get hurt, which we will, they tell us to wait for the doctor as we bleed out on the factory floor!"

Everyone nodded in agreement. Sarah noticed six workers standing slightly apart, their few possessions bundled at their feet. Tommy's factory badge was conspicuously missing.

"What happened?" Sarah asked the woman beside her.

"They've been locked out," the woman whispered. "Thorne caught them with the petition during lunch break. Called it 'agitation' and barred them from entry."

"Bailey thinks he can pick us off one by one," Tommy continued, pounding his fist into his palm.

"What does he expect us to do?" someone called out. "Starve?"

"That's exactly what he expects," Tommy replied.

"But we won't. We can't strike, not yet, but we can make our voices heard in other ways."

A tall, broad-shouldered man pushed through the crowd. Sarah recognized him as one of Bailey's new security men, hired after the Northern Review article. Two others followed close behind.

"This gathering is unauthorized," the man announced. "Disperse immediately."

Tommy stood his ground. "We're on public ground outside the mill property. We've every right to be here."

"Not if you're inciting unrest." The security man stepped closer, his hand moving to the truncheon at his belt. "Mr. Bailey has authorized us to maintain order by any means necessary."

"We're just talking," Tommy countered. "Last I checked that wasn't against the law."

The security man smiled unpleasantly. "Funny how troublemakers always say that right before trouble starts."

Sarah saw his grip tighten on the truncheon. Without thinking, she moved to Tommy's side.

"Leave him alone," she said. "He hasn't done anything wrong."

The security man's gaze flicked to her. "Another

one. You mill girls should learn to keep your mouths shut."

"And you should learn some manners," Sarah shot back.

His face darkened. "Maybe you need a lesson in respect."

He pulled the truncheon free in one smooth motion, raising it toward Sarah. She stood frozen, realizing too late she'd pushed too far.

Tommy lunged between them, shouting, "Look out!"

The truncheon connected with a sickening crack, not against Sarah's head, but against Tommy's. He crumpled to the ground as screams erupted from the crowd.

"Tommy!" Sarah dropped to her knees beside him.

The workers surged forward, shouting in anger, and the security men pushed back, their truncheons now fully drawn. Someone threw a rock, and it barely missed one of Bailey's men.

"Stop!" Sarah shouted, her hands pressed to Tommy's bleeding head. "This won't help!"

The police whistle rang and within seconds, the security men backed away, and the workers scattered, not willing to risk arrest.

"Tommy," Sarah patted his cheek. "Can you hear me?"

His eyelids fluttered. "Did I save the day?"

"You idiot," Sarah whispered. "Can you stand?"

"Probably not," Tommy said, attempting a grin that turned into a grimace. "But for you, I'll try."

With Sarah's help, Tommy struggled to his feet, swaying dangerously. Blood trickled from a gash above his temple.

"We need to get him to a doctor," Sarah said to the few workers who remained.

"Can't afford one," Tommy mumbled. "Take me to Aunt Bess."

"Mrs. Winters it is," Sarah agreed. "Can someone help me?"

Two men stepped forward, supporting Tommy between them. Together, they made their way through back streets, avoiding the police who'd arrived to disperse the remainder of the gathering.

Mrs. Winters' shop was closed, but smoke curled from the chimney of the attached house. Sarah knocked urgently.

Annie opened the door, her welcoming smile vanishing at the sight of Tommy's bloodied face.

"Oh my God," she gasped. "What happened?"

"Bailey's men," Sarah explained as they maneuvered Tommy inside. "He got in the way of a truncheon meant for me."

"Always acting the hero," Annie muttered, but her hands were gentle as she helped lower Tommy onto the sofa.

Mrs. Winters appeared from the kitchen, her face paling at the sight of her nephew. "Tommy! Saints preserve us!"

"It's just a scratch, Aunt Bess," Tommy slurred, blinking blood from his eye.

"A scratch wouldn't leave you looking like Sunday's slaughterhouse special," Mrs. Winters snapped, but her hands trembled as she examined the wound. "Annie, fetch my medicine box. Sarah, water and clean cloths."

They hurried to obey, leaving Mrs. Winters muttering dire predictions about Tommy's future if he continued "poking sticks at the Bailey beehive."

In the kitchen, Annie pumped water furiously into a basin.

"When will he learn?" she asked, voice tight with fear. "When will he understand he can't fight them all by himself?"

"He wasn't by himself," Sarah said quietly. "He was protecting me."

Annie's pumping slowed. "Of course he was."

Sarah gathered clean rags from the drawer while Annie added herbs to the water.

"He's locked out of the mill," Sarah told her. "Thorne caught him with the petition."

"Locked out?" Annie stared at her. "But his contract…"

"Apparently means nothing when Bailey wants someone gone."

They returned to find Mrs. Winters cleaning Tommy's wound while he tried unsuccessfully to bat her hands away.

"Stay still, you ridiculous boy," she scolded. "Or I'll tie you down like I did when you had chicken pox at nine."

"You wouldn't," Tommy protested weakly.

"Try me."

Sarah and Annie set their supplies beside Mrs. Winters, who immediately began grinding herbs into a paste.

"Hold this against the cut," she instructed Annie. "Press it firmly."

Annie took the cloth and leaned over Tommy. "Like this?"

"Perfect." Mrs. Winters nodded.

Tommy grinned up at Annie "Worry not. I've got

a strong head. Who knew my thick skull would finally prove useful?"

"This isn't funny," Annie said, but her voice wobbled.

"It is a little funny," Tommy insisted. "It took a truncheon to the head to get you to talk to me again."

"I was already talking to you," Annie retorted, pressing perhaps a bit harder than necessary.

"Ow! Careful with your ministrations, Florence Nightingale." Tommy winced. "I'm a delicate patient in need of gentle care."

"You're a troublemaker in need of sense," Annie countered, though her touch softened.

"If I'm dying…"

"You're not dying," all three women said in unison.

"…I want it noted that I've always thought Annie Parker was the prettiest girl in Lancashire," Tommy continued, "and I've been half in love with her since she shared her bread with me on her first day at the mill."

Annie's cheeks flushed crimson. "You're delirious from the blow."

"Probably," Tommy agreed cheerfully. "But no less truthful for it."

Mrs. Winters finished preparing her herbal paste

and moved to apply it to Tommy's wound. "Sarah, would you fetch the whiskey? The good bottle, in the top cabinet."

Sarah nodded, recognizing the request for what it was, a chance to give Tommy and Annie a moment alone. She retreated to the kitchen, taking her time finding the bottle and pouring a small measure into a cup.

When she returned, Annie was still bent over Tommy, but they'd fallen silent, staring at each other with matching expressions of wonder and uncertainty.

Sarah cleared her throat. "The whiskey."

They startled apart. Mrs. Winters took the cup with a knowing smile.

"Tommy needs rest now," she announced. "Sarah, help me prepare a poultice for later. Annie can keep him company."

"I don't need…" Tommy began.

"You two," Sarah interrupted firmly, "need to talk. Properly."

"Sarah!" Annie protested.

"She's right," Mrs. Winters agreed. "Life's too short for dancing around your feelings, especially in times like these."

Sarah followed Mrs. Winters to the kitchen,

leaving Tommy and Annie in awkward silence behind them. Through the partly open door, she heard Tommy say softly, "I really am sorry, Annie. For everything."

"I know," Annie replied. "Just... don't die on me, all right?"

"I wouldn't dream of it. Who else would annoy you so consistently?"

Their voices dropped too low to hear after that. Mrs. Winters smiled as she pulled herbs from various jars.

"Finally," she murmured. "I was beginning to think they'd never sort themselves out."

"Sometimes it takes a near death experience," Sarah said, thinking of Daniel's letter and feeling a fresh wave of misery.

Mrs. Winters studied her face. "You look like you've had a day, my girl."

"It's been..." Sarah trailed off, not knowing where to begin. "Difficult."

"Sit." Mrs. Winters gestured to the kitchen chair. "Nothing to be done for my nephew that isn't already happening. Tell me."

Sarah sank into the chair, suddenly exhausted. "A girl lost her fingers in the knotter's room today.

Thorne wanted to make her wait hours for the doctor."

"Ahhh. Monsters, the lot of them," Mrs. Winters muttered. "Did she get help?"

"Eventually. I insisted, so Thorne dismissed me without pay for two days."

"For insisting an injured girl see a doctor?" Mrs. Winters shook her head in disgust. "And they wonder why workers want to organize a strike."

"Bailey also implemented a new stretching system to have four stations per worker instead of two."

"That's what caused the accident?"

"Partly. Lily was exhausted and still trying to manage too many tasks at once."

Mrs. Winters sighed heavily, her usual animation fading. "It gets worse, I'm afraid. My friend Martha visited earlier and she's a chambermaid for the Westmoreland's. She says all the mill owners are requiring workers to sign an agreement."

"What kind of agreement?"

"A pledge denouncing the unions and any collective action," Mrs. Winters said grimly. "Anyone who refuses to sign loses their position immediately, with no references, and no final wages."

Sarah stared at her. "They can't do that."

"They can do whatever they like, my dear. Who's to stop them?" Mrs. Winters patted Sarah's hand. "Bailey's implementing it next week, according to Martha. Every worker must sign or leave."

"And they expect Tommy and the others to crawl back and sign after being locked out?"

"That's exactly what they expect." Mrs. Winters' eyes hardened. "Break the strongest ones first, make examples of them, and then the rest will fall in line."

"What do we do?"

Mrs. Winters squeezed her hand. "We survive, my girl. We bend when we must and stand firm when we can. And we remember that even the strongest storm eventually passes."

"Tommy won't sign," Sarah said with certainty. "He'd rather starve."

"Yes, well, my nephew has more courage than sense sometimes," Mrs. Winters agreed with a sad smile. "But he's tougher than he looks. He takes after my side of the family."

They fell silent, and Sarah closed her eyes briefly, imagining she lived in a different world.

"What's troubling you, Sarah?" Mrs. Winters asked gently. "There's more, isn't there?"

Sarah opened her eyes. "Nothing important."

"Hmm." Mrs. Winters didn't press, but her

knowing gaze suggested she understood more than Sarah had said. "Well, you're welcome to stay here tonight. I won't have you walking back to that dormitory in the dark with Bailey's thugs about."

"Thank you," Sarah said, grateful beyond words for the simple kindness.

From the other room came the surprising sound of Annie's laughter, followed by Tommy's deeper chuckle.

"Well," Mrs. Winters smiled, "some good has come of today at least."

Sarah nodded, trying to summon happiness for her friends despite the hollow ache in her chest. Tommy and Annie had found each other.

Some barriers, it seemed, could be broken after all.

Just not the ones that mattered to her.

# CHAPTER 23

*D*aniel

DANIEL PACED his bedroom like a caged animal. It's been four days since his father's ultimatum, three since the engagement announcement appeared in the papers, and still no word from Sarah. Had Arthur delivered his letter? Had she read it? The questions chased each other around his mind until he thought he might go mad.

A soft knock interrupted his brooding.

"Enter," he called, expecting Arthur with his evening tea.

Instead, his mother slipped inside, closing the door quietly behind her. "Daniel."

"Mother." He straightened, surprised. Elizabeth Bailey rarely visited his rooms, especially not after dark. "Is everything all right?"

"No," she said simply. "Nothing is all right, and I think you know that."

She moved to the window, peering out at the distant mill silhouetted against the night sky. "Your father has gone to Manchester for two days with Mr. Harringtons."

"Wedding plans, no doubt," Daniel said bitterly.

"Among other things." Elizabeth turned to face him. "This may be our only chance to speak freely."

Daniel gestured for her to sit in the armchair by the fireplace, taking the opposite seat. "What's happening at the mill? Arthur says there's been trouble."

"Your father calls it 'maintaining order.'" Elizabeth's mouth tightened. "Six workers were barred for circulating a petition. A girl lost two fingers in the new stretching system. And soon, every worker must sign a pledge denouncing the unions or lose their positions."

"He can't do that."

"He already has." Elizabeth leaned forward,.

"Daniel, this isn't just about Bailey's Mill anymore. The Northern Review has published three more articles and the parliament is beginning to take notice."

Daniel sat up straighter. "Parliament?"

"There's talk of a formal inquiry into the working conditions in Lancashire mills." Elizabeth reached into her sleeve and withdrew a folded letter. "My cousin Henry sits on the committee."

"Lord Ashworth is your cousin? You never mentioned..."

"There are many things I've never mentioned," Elizabeth interrupted. "Including that Henry and I have corresponded for years." She handed him the letter. "He wants to speak with you."

Daniel unfolded the paper, scanning its contents with growing excitement. "He wants me to testify about Father's practices?"

"You have firsthand knowledge that no worker could provide," Elizabeth said. "The account books, the accident reports, the wage calculations are evidence Henry's committee needs."

"Father would never forgive me." Daniel looked up from the letter. "This would be the final break between us."

"I know." Elizabeth's eyes softened. "Which is why

I can't tell you what to do. This must be your decision alone."

Daniel stood, crossing to his desk where Bailey Mill's quarterly reports lay hidden beneath other papers. "It's not really a decision, Mother. Not anymore." He turned to face her. "I can't keep living with myself if I do nothing."

"Then we must get you to London immediately, while your father is away. Henry can arrange safe lodging until the committee convenes."

"I'll need to gather the evidence." Daniel gestured to the reports.

"Arthur can help arrange what you need." Elizabeth rose, suddenly all business. "Pack only essentials. The carriage will be ready at dawn."

"Wait," Daniel said, a thought striking him. "I need to see Sarah first."

"The mill girl?" Elizabeth's brow furrowed. "Daniel, that's too risky. Your father has men watching for you at the mill gates."

"I have to know she's all right." Daniel ran a hand through his hair. "Mother, Father threatened to destroy her if I didn't comply with the marriage. What if he's already acted on that threat?"

Elizabeth studied her son's face. "You truly care for her."

"I do." Daniel didn't bother hiding it anymore. "More than I should, more than it makes any sense."

"Love rarely makes sense," Elizabeth said softly. "Very well. We'll delay departure until midday. That should give you time to visit the mill before we leave for London."

"Thank you mother" Daniel took his mother's hands.

"I understand more than you know." Elizabeth squeezed his hands. "Now get some rest. Tomorrow will change everything, one way or another."

After she left, Daniel sat at his desk and began sorting through the reports and selecting those that showed the most damning evidence of his father's practices. By dawn, he had compiled a portfolio that told a clear story of exploitation and disregard for workers' safety.

Arthur arrived with breakfast and news that the carriage was being prepared for a "shopping trip" to Manchester - the story Elizabeth had given the household staff.

"Your mother says to meet her at noon by the east gate," Arthur reported, helping Daniel pack a small valise. "The driver has been well paid for his discretion."

"And what about you, Arthur?" Daniel asked. "My

father will be furious when he discovers your role in this."

"I've already handed in my notice, sir." Arthur straightened, an uncharacteristic smile playing at his lips.

Daniel blinked in surprise. "What would you do?."
"I'll survive,"

By mid-morning, Daniel was ready. He slipped from the house unnoticed while the servants were occupied with their daily tasks. Instead of heading to the east gate where he would later meet his mother, he made his way toward the mill.

Even from a distance, he could tell something was wrong. A crowd had gathered outside the gates, not just a few workers, but hundreds, spilling into the streets surrounding the mill. The factory chimneys stood silent, and no smoke was billowing from them.

A strike. It had finally happened.

Daniel pulled his cap lower over his eyes, moving carefully through the crowd. Workers stood in tight groups. Some held crude signs demanding fair wages and safety measures. Others handed out soup and bread to families already feeling the pinch of lost wages.

He spotted Mr. Thorne at the gates, red-faced

and shouting at a group of men who appeared to be strike organizers. Security men flanked him, truncheons at the ready.

"...will all be dismissed without reference!" Thorne was saying. "Mr. Bailey will not tolerate this insubordination!"

"We're not asking for tolerance," a familiar voice responded. Tommy Briggs, sporting a bandaged head but standing tall. "We're demanding basic human dignity."

Daniel continued through the crowd, searching for Sarah. He passed women comforting crying children, men with faces hardened by years of labor, and young boys trying to look brave despite their obvious fear.

Sarah stood near the back of the crowd, distributing what looked like pamphlets to workers. Her face was pale, and she was thinner than he remembered, the bones of her wrist was sharp beneath her skin as she handed papers to an elderly knotter.

Daniel moved toward her, and when he was just a few feet away, she looked up, and her eyes widened.

Before she could speak, or worse, call out his name, Daniel grasped her elbow and pulled her gently but firmly away from the crowd.

"What are you…" she began, trying to wrench her arm free.

"Please," Daniel said quietly. "Just come with me. It's important."

Something in his voice must have convinced her, because she stopped resisting, though her body remained tense under his touch. He led her away from the main gates, down a side street, and toward the small library.

"The mill is closed," she said flatly as he unlocked the library door. "Shouldn't you be at home preparing for your wedding?"

Daniel winced at the bitterness in her voice. He ushered her inside and closed the door behind them, and finally released her arm.

"Are you all right?" he asked, studying her face.

"I'm fine." Sarah stepped away from him, creating distance between them. "Is that why you pulled me away from the strike? To check if I'm all right?"

"Partly." Daniel removed his cap. "And to explain about the engagement announcement."

"There's nothing to explain." Sarah's voice was cool. "Congratulations on your upcoming nuptials, Mr. Bailey. I'm sure you and Miss Harrington will be very happy together."

"Sarah, please…"

"Are you enjoying this?" she interrupted, her composure cracking slightly. "Did it amuse you to toy with me while you were arranging your marriage to a woman of your own class?"

Daniel stared at her, bewildered. "Toy with you? Sarah, I've never…"

"Your letter made your feelings perfectly clear." Sarah crossed her arms over her chest. "Though I must say, I expected at least the courtesy of a face-to-face dismissal."

"My letter?" Daniel shook his head. "What are you talking about?"

Sarah's eyes narrowed. "Don't pretend to be ignorant. It's beneath even you."

"I genuinely don't know what letter you mean," Daniel insisted. "I wrote to explain about the engagement announcement, that it was my father's doing, not mine. That I had no intention of marrying Catherine."

"That's not what your letter said." Sarah's voice was flat. "Your letter called our friendship a 'momentary curiosity' and ordered me never to contact you again."

Daniel felt the blood drain from his face. "I never wrote that. Never."

Something in his expression must have reached her because uncertainty flickered across her face.

"The letter was with a book," she said. "'Pride and Prejudice.' You left it in our usual spot."

Daniel moved to the window seat where they'd exchanged books and letters. "Show me. Please."

Sarah hesitated, then reached into her pocket and withdrew a folded paper. Daniel took it and read.

His stomach turned with each cold, dismissive line. A momentary curiosity. A pleasant diversion. A man in my position must maintain certain standards.

"I didn't write this," he said when he finished, "This isn't my handwriting, though it's a good forgery."

"Then who..." Sarah's eyes widened in understanding. "Your father?"

"He's probably intercepted our correspondence." Daniel crumpled the letter in his fist. "He threatened to have you dismissed if I didn't go through with the marriage to Catherine."

Sarah sank onto the window seat. "So he wrote this to make sure I'd stay away from you."

"I'm so sorry, Sarah." Daniel moved toward her but stopped short of touching her. "I would never say these things to you. I would never think of you that way."

She looked up at him. "I believe you," she said finally. "But it changes nothing, Daniel."

"It changes everything," he countered. "My father tried to separate us because he knows how I feel about you."

"And how is that?" Sarah asked quietly.

Daniel took a deep breath. "I care for you, Sarah. More than I've cared for anyone. When I'm with you, I feel... like the person I'm meant to be, not the person my father wants me to be."

"That's just it, isn't it?" Sarah stood again. "Who you're meant to be and who I am can never align. Not in this world."

"We could try..."

"And face what consequences?" Sarah shook her head. "Your father would destroy both of us. The workers need you as an ally, not a cautionary tale."

"I'm leaving for London today," Daniel said. "My mother's cousin sits on a parliamentary committee investigating mill conditions. I'm going to testify against my father."

Sarah stared at him. "You'd do that?"

"I have to." Daniel stepped closer. "I can't keep living with myself otherwise. And after that... after that, things will change. I'll have no inheritance, no position, but I'll be free."

"Free to do what? Marry a knotter with nothing to her name?" Sarah laughed sadly. "Be realistic, Daniel."

"I am being realistic," he insisted. "For the first time in my life."

Sarah touched his cheek briefly. "You're a good man, Daniel Bailey. Better than your father ever was. But we exist in different worlds."

"Worlds can change."

"Not quickly enough." Sarah dropped her hand. "Not for us."

"Sarah, please." Daniel caught her fingers before she could pull away completely. "Come with me to London. We can start fresh somewhere my father can't reach you."

"And what about the others?" She gestured toward the windows, where the strike continued outside. "Tommy, Annie, Mrs. Fletcher? I can't abandon them to face your father's wrath alone."

Daniel knew he was losing her. "Then wait for me. I'll come back after the committee hearing."

"To what end?" Sarah asked gently. "A few more stolen moments in this library before reality intrudes again? I care for you too much to pretend we have a future, Daniel."

"So that's it? We just... give up?"

"We accept what is," Sarah corrected. "You go to London. You tell the truth about the mills. You make a difference for hundreds of workers. And I stay here, or go anywhere that fits my world."

Daniel felt as if the floor were tilting beneath him. "I don't want to lose you."

"Maybe in another life," Sarah said softly. "One where you weren't born a Bailey, and I wasn't born an orphan. One where the distance between us wasn't an uncrossable chasm."

She stepped back, and this time he let her go. "Goodbye, Daniel. Do what you need to do in London. Make it count."

"Sarah..."

But she was already moving toward the door, her back straight and head high.

"Be careful at the strike," he said, the words inadequate even to his own ears. "My father's men won't show mercy."

"Neither will we," Sarah replied, pausing at the door. "Good luck in London."

## CHAPTER 24

*Sarah*

THE SECOND DAY of the strike brought heavy rain that drummed against Mrs. Winters' kitchen windows. The small room felt crowded but warm, a welcome refuge from the soggy picket lines outside Bailey's Mill. Sarah sat at the worn wooden table, nursing a cup of tea while Tommy poked at his bandaged head.

"Stop touching it," Annie scolded, slapping his hand away. "You'll make it worse."

"It itches," Tommy complained. "How's a man

supposed to heal with an itchy bandage driving him mad?"

"You could try sitting still for more than ten seconds," Mrs. Winters suggested, stirring a pot of stew that filled the kitchen with rich, savory smells. "Though I realize that might be asking for the impossible."

It's been two days since Thorne had posted the notice requiring all workers to sign the anti-union pledge. Two days since she and Tommy had refused and found themselves officially dismissed from Bailey's Mill.

"So," Tommy said, leaning back in his chair despite Annie's disapproving look, "that's it then. Three years at Bailey's, and all I have to show for it is this impressive head wound and no reference."

"You don't sound very upset about it," Sarah observed.

Tommy grinned. "Why would I be? We've started something bigger than ourselves." He gestured toward the window where rain streamed down the glass. "Two hundred workers on strike. The Northern Review sent a reporter. Even the London papers are writing about Bailey's Mill now."

"That doesn't put food on your plate," Mrs.

Winters pointed out practically, though her eyes shone with pride.

"True," Tommy conceded. "But for once, it feels like we're doing something that matters. Like maybe we're not just cogs in Bailey's machine after all."

"What will you do now?" Annie asked quietly. "Both of you?"

Sarah stared into her teacup, avoiding everyone's eyes. Her entire existence had revolved around the mill, its routines, its demands, and its walls defined the boundaries of her world. Now that world had vanished.

"Well," Mrs. Winters said, turning from the stove with a decisive air. "That's something I've been meaning to discuss with all of you."

She wiped her hands on her apron and joined them at the table. "I've decided to sell the bakery."

"What?" Tommy straightened, wincing as the sudden movement jarred his injury. "Aunt Bess, you can't!"

"I most certainly can," Mrs. Winters replied calmly. "Margaret Simmons has been after me to sell for years. She's offered a fair price, and I've accepted."

"But the shop has been yours for fifteen years," Tommy protested. "You love it here."

"I loved it here," Mrs. Winters corrected. "Past tense. Lancashire isn't what it used to be." She looked at each of them in turn. "I'm moving to Manchester. And I'd like all of you to come with me."

"Manchester?" Annie was the first to recover. "But that's so far."

"Thirty miles is hardly the end of the earth," Mrs. Winters said dryly. "And Manchester has opportunities Lancashire can't offer anymore. Especially for three young people blacklisted by Edward Bailey."

"We can't impose on you like that," Sarah said softly.

"Impose?" Mrs. Winters snorted. "Who's imposing? I'm being entirely selfish. I'm too old to start over alone in a new city. I need young backs and strong hands to help me."

"Aunt Bess," Tommy began.

"Don't 'Aunt Bess' me with those puppy dog eyes," Mrs. Winters cut him off. "I've made up my mind. I've put a deposit on a little shop with living quarters above it. Bigger than this place, with a proper kitchen for baking."

"What would we do there?" Sarah asked, unable to keep the doubt from her voice. "None of us have skills beyond mill work."

"Nonsense." Mrs. Winters tapped the table for

emphasis. "Annie has already proven herself a natural baker. The girl has magic in her hands when it comes to pastry."

Annie blushed at the praise.

"Sarah, you've got the neatest stitches I've ever seen," Mrs. Winters continued. "Those handkerchiefs you make could sell well in a city shop. You could learn dressmaking, and millinery. Plenty of seamstresses would take on an apprentice with your eye for detail."

"And me?" Tommy asked, raising an eyebrow. "What hidden talents have you discovered in your troublemaking nephew?"

"You," Mrs. Winters said, "can learn to fix things. Manchester is full of machines that need maintaining. You've always had a knack for understanding how things work, why else could you sabotage Bailey's machines so effectively?"

Tommy's jaw dropped. "You knew about that?"

"Please." Mrs. Winters rolled her eyes. "I raised you, boy. You couldn't keep a secret from me when you were ten, and you can't now."

Sarah let out a small laugh. "You've got it all figured out, haven't you?"

"I've had plenty of time to think while watching you three fumble around each other," Mrs. Winters replied. "The way I see it, we could all start fresh. And maybe, after we're established, open our own little shops."

"I don't know," Sarah said hesitantly. "It sounds wonderful, but we'd be depending on your charity. That's not right."

"It's not charity to help family," Mrs. Winters said firmly. "And like it or not, you three are family to me now."

Tommy reached for Annie's hand across the table. "What do you think? You're already working with Aunt Bess here..."

Annie bit her lip. "I do love the baking. And there's nothing for us in Lancashire anymore, is there? Not with Bailey's men watching the strike and taking names."

"They'll never hire any of us back," Sarah agreed. "Not after everything that's happened."

"Then it's settled," Mrs. Winters declared, returning to her stew pot. "We'll leave at the end of the month. That gives me time to finalize the sale and all of you time to tie up any loose ends here."

"That's barely two weeks," Sarah protested.

"Best to move quickly before Bailey and his kind find new ways to make life difficult." Mrs. Winters began ladling stew into bowls. "Now eat."

After dinner, Tommy insisted on helping Mrs. Winters with the dishes despite his injury, leaving Sarah and Annie to step outside for fresh air. The rain had stopped, and the small back garden was damp but peaceful in the evening light.

They sat on the back step, shoulders touching companionably.

"Manchester," Annie said finally, testing the word. "It seems so far away."

"Thirty miles isn't the end of the earth," Sarah quoted Mrs. Winters with a smile. "Or so I've been told."

"It might as well be another country." Annie plucked at her skirt. "I've never been more than five miles from where I was born."

"Me neither," Sarah admitted. "It's terrifying. And also..."

"Exciting?" Annie finished for her.

"Yes." Sarah was surprised to realize it was true. "A place where no one knows us or what we've been through. Where we can be something other than mill girls."

"Or former mill girls," Annie corrected with a small laugh. She glanced back toward the kitchen window, where Tommy's animated silhouette was visible. "Tommy seems happy about it, at least."

"Tommy would be happy about moving to the moon if you were going with him," Sarah teased.

Annie's cheeks flushed pink. "Don't be ridiculous."

"Oh? So, you two haven't been making eyes at each other over Mrs. Winters' baking table for the past week?"

"Sarah!" Annie's blush deepened, but she couldn't hide her smile. "It's not... we haven't... it's still new."

"But it is something?" Sarah nudged her gently.

Annie nodded, suddenly shy. "He asked if he could court me properly. He'd been half in love with me since my first day at the mill, can you believe it?"

"Easily," Sarah replied. "Anyone with eyes could see it."

"He's different when we're alone," Annie said softly. "He's still Tommy, still ridiculous and full of big ideas, but gentler too. He talks about the future like it's something we'll share."

"And will you? Share it, I mean."

"I think so." Annie's smile widened. "He makes me laugh, even when everything is terrible. That's worth something, isn't it?"

"It's worth everything," Sarah agreed, genuinely happy for her friend. "You deserve someone who makes you laugh, Annie."

Annie studied Sarah's face. "And what about you? Any mill boys catch your fancy before... well, before everything fell apart?"

Sarah looked away. "No. No mill boys."

Something in her tone made Annie lean closer. "But there was someone," she said. It wasn't a question.

Sarah remained silent, watching a sparrow hop along the garden wall.

"Sarah Dobbs," Annie said with sudden realization, "you're hiding something. You've never been able to lie to me."

"It's nothing. It was nothing." Sarah hugged her knees to her chest. "A silly dream, that's all."

"Tell me," Annie urged gently. "Please? After everything we've been through, you can trust me with anything."

The words bubbled up before Sarah could stop them. "It was Daniel Bailey."

Annie's mouth fell open. "Daniel Bailey? The mill owner's son?"

Sarah nodded miserably.

"But how? When? Where?"

"The library," Sarah admitted. "We started talking about books. Then we exchanged letters. We were just having conversations at first. Nothing improper."

"And then?"

"And then it wasn't just that anymore." Sarah plucked at a loose thread on her sleeve. "At least, not for me."

"Oh, Sarah." Annie's voice was soft with understanding. "That's why you've been different since the engagement announcement."

"I knew nothing could ever happen between us," Sarah continued, "He's Daniel Bailey and I'm nobody. But for a little while, when we were just talking about books, it felt like those things didn't matter."

"Did he... I mean, did he feel the same?"

"I thought he might," Sarah said. "Then came the engagement announcement and a horrible letter. But it wasn't from him, it was his father's doing. Daniel found me during the strike and explained everything."

"What did he say?"

"That he cares for me. That he's going to London to testify against his father to a parliamentary committee. That he wanted me to go with him." Sarah laughed bitterly. "As if it were that simple."

"And you said no."

"What else could I say? Yes, I'll run away with the mill owner's son and destroy both our lives?" Sarah shook her head. "There's no future there, Annie."

To Sarah's horror, tears began sliding down her cheeks. She wiped them away angrily, but more followed.

"I'm so stupid," she whispered. "To think someone like him could ever truly care for someone like me."

"Stop that," Annie said firmly, wrapping an arm around Sarah's shoulders. "You're not stupid. And if he truly cares for you, it's because he sees what I see. That you're the strongest, smartest, most loyal friend anyone could have."

"It doesn't matter what he sees," Sarah said, her voice breaking. "We're from different worlds."

"Worlds can change," Annie said softly.

"Not quickly enough. Not for us." Sarah leaned into her friend's embrace. "And now I'm leaving for Manchester and he's going to London and that's the way it has to be."

Annie said nothing, simply holding Sarah as she cried for the impossible dream—for stolen conversations in a dusty library, for the brief, beautiful moments when class and circumstance hadn't mattered, for the future that could never be.

"I hate this," Sarah said finally, when the tears had

subsided. "I hate that I'm crying over a man. That's not who I am."

"You're crying over an unfair world," Annie corrected. "There's no shame in that."

Sarah straightened, wiping her face with her sleeve. "It doesn't matter now. Manchester is waiting, and whatever I felt for Daniel Bailey stays here in Lancashire."

"If you say so," Annie said, clearly unconvinced.

"I do." Sarah forced a smile. "Now tell me more about you and Tommy. Does he still say ridiculous things when you're alone, or does he suddenly become a poet?".

## CHAPTER 25

### Daniel

DANIEL SAT ramrod straight at the parliamentary committee room and across from him, twelve men in expensive suits gazed down from their elevated platform, their expressions ranging from boredom to mild interest.

"Mr. Bailey," Lord Ashworth began, consulting his notes, "you claim that Lancashire mills routinely operate outside safety regulations. Can you provide specific examples?"

Daniel opened the accident ledger. "I've compiled records from six major mills, including my father's.

In the past year alone, these mills reported one hundred and forty-seven severe machinery accidents. Ninety-three involved children under sixteen. In most cases, injured workers waited hours for medical attention, if they received any at all."

"And your evidence for this?" asked a jowly man to Ashworth's right.

"The' own records, sir." Daniel indicated the open ledger. "These are copies of official accident reports, signed by mill physicians. You'll note the time of injury and time of treatment are recorded. In this case..." he pointed to an entry "...an eight-year-old boy lost three fingers at nine in the morning but received no medical care until four in the afternoon."

"These are unfortunate incidents," another committee member said dismissively. "But accidents happen in any industrial setting. Surely you're not suggesting mill owners deliberately delay medical care?"

"I am precisely suggesting that" Daniel replied firmly. "Standard policy in most Lancashire mills states that physicians visit only at specific hours daily. Any worker injured must wait, regardless of severity."

Lord Ashworth leaned forward. "And the

'stretching system' you mentioned in your written statement?"

"It was implemented across the region last month." Daniel opened another ledger. "The workers previously managed two stations each. Now they're required to manage four, covering twice the physical distance while maintaining the same production quotas."

"A reasonable efficiency measure," the jowly man interjected. "Economic pressures demand adaptation."

"The day after implementation at one mill, a fifteen-year-old girl lost two fingers because she was rushing between stations," Daniel countered. "When a knotter insisted she receive immediate medical attention, she was dismissed without pay."

"Let us move to wages," Ashworth suggested. "You've provided some rather disturbing calculations."

Daniel pulled forward another ledger. "Lancashire mills have cut wages three times in the past year, totaling a twenty-five percent reduction. Meanwhile, industry profits have increased by an average of eighteen percent."

He distributed copies of a chart to each committee member. "This indicates the current weekly wage for different mill positions compared to basic living costs in Lancashire. As you can see, even working six days a week, no mill worker earns enough to afford adequate food, housing, and coal."

"Business operations must respond to market pressures," a thin, spectacled man remarked. "These adjustments affect the entire industry."

"That doesn't make it right," Daniel said sharply. "Nor does it justify a fine system that further reduces wages for infractions as minor as coughing on the factory floor."

"You paint a grim picture, Mr. Bailey," Lord Ashworth observed. "But I'm curious... why come forward now? These practices have presumably been ongoing throughout your life."

Daniel hesitated. "Because I've seen the human cost," he said finally. "I've met the children working sixteen-hour shifts. I've spoken with women who can't feed their families despite working six days a week. I've watched workers suffer preventable injuries while overseers worried about production quotas."

He closed the ledger before him. "I've benefited from these practices my entire life without questioning them. That makes me complicit. I can't change the past, but I can ensure that the truth is known now."

Ashworth nodded thoughtfully. "What are you proposing, exactly?"

Daniel sat straighter. "A formal investigation of all Lancashire mills, followed by enforceable regulations on working hours, minimum wages, and safety requirements. Particular attention should be paid to child labor practices. This isn't about one mill or one owner, it's about an entire system that sacrifices human lives for profit."

"That's quite a sweeping indictment," the jowly man said coldly. "Many on this committee have manufacturing interests. Are you suggesting we're all callous profiteers?"

"I'm suggesting that without regulatory oversight, economic pressures push even well-intentioned owners toward exploitative practices," Daniel replied carefully. "The solution must be industry-wide standards that protect workers while allowing businesses to compete fairly."

"And if these regulations make British textiles unable to compete with foreign manufacturers?" another member asked.

"Then we must ask ourselves what price we're willing to pay for economic dominance," Daniel said.

Only Ashworth seemed genuinely troubled by Daniel's evidence.

"The committee will consider all testimony presented today," Ashworth announced eventually. "We will issue our recommendations within the month."

As the committee filed out, Daniel gathered his documents, his hands shaking slightly from the tension of the past hours. The Northern Review journalist who'd helped him prepare his testimony approached.

"Well done, Bailey," Norton said, shaking his hand. "You gave them more than they bargained for."

"Will it make any difference?" Daniel asked.

"Hard to say." Norton gestured to his notebook. "But every word you said is going in tomorrow's edition. Sometimes public opinion can accomplish what committees won't."

Lord Ashworth approached as the room emptied. "You've started something important today," he said. "Though change comes slowly in these matters."

"Too slowly for those suffering now," Daniel replied.

"Indeed." Ashworth hesitated. "I should warn you, word of your testimony will reach Lancashire before you do. Your father's associates were taking notes, and none looked pleased."

Daniel nodded, unsurprised. "I knew the consequences when I agreed to testify."

"Your mother asked me to give you this." Ashworth passed Daniel a sealed letter. "She feared you might need it sooner than expected."

Daniel tucked the letter into his jacket. "Thank you, my lord."

"Where will you go now?" Ashworth asked.

Daniel realized he had no answer. "I don't know," he admitted. "Not London. Perhaps back to Lancashire first, to settle matters."

"Be careful," Ashworth warned. "You've made powerful enemies today, including some who may wish to prevent your return altogether."

* * *

THREE DAYS LATER, Daniel stepped off the London train at a small station fifteen miles from Lancashire. Lord Ashworth had arranged for a private carriage to meet him, driven by a trusted servant who knew the back roads to the Bailey estate.

"We must hurry, sir," the driver whispered as Daniel boarded. "Your man Evans says security has been tightened since word of your testimony reached Mr. Bailey."

They traveled taking winding country lanes to avoid the main roads where they might be recognized. The carriage stopped at last in a small copse of trees behind the Bailey property.

Arthur waited there, his face drawn with worry.

"Sir," he greeted Daniel quietly. "We haven't much time."

"What's happened, Arthur?" Daniel asked, climbing down from the carriage.

"Your father received telegrams from London yesterday. He..." Arthur hesitated. "He was not pleased. He's ordered the staff to remove all your possessions from the house and burn anything left behind by nightfall."

Daniel winced but wasn't surprised. "What about my mother?"

"She's arranged to meet you at St. Mark's Church at noon," Arthur replied. "I've prepared a separate carriage with your belongings."

"You've risked a great deal," Daniel observed.

"As have you, sir." Arthur led him through the trees to where a modest carriage waited, loaded with trunks. "Everything I could salvage is here."

"Arthur, you shouldn't…"

"It's already done," Arthur interrupted. "And I've been dismissed for my trouble. Excessive loyalty to the wrong Bailey, apparently."

Daniel's face fell. "I never intended…"

"No apologies necessary," Arthur said firmly. "I made my choice freely, as did you." He checked his pocket watch. "We should go. Your father has men watching the main roads."

They traveled carefully through back lanes, the carriage springs protesting against Lancashire's rough country roads. Daniel opened his mother's letter, reading her elegant handwriting by the dim carriage lantern.

*My dearest Daniel,*

*If Lord Ashworth has given you this letter, then you have taken your stand. I am prouder than I can express, though I fear what awaits you here.*

*Your father will not forgive what he sees as betrayal. You must be prepared for the worst. I have arranged a small account at Marshall's Bank in Manchester… my own inheritance, kept separate from your father's fortune. The details are enclosed.*

*I will try to see you once more before you must leave Lancashire. Until then, know that you carry my love and pride with you always.*

*Your loving mother*

Enclosed was a small bank book showing a very sufficient sum.

St. Mark's Church was quiet when Arthur pulled the carriage to a stop.

"I'll wait with your belongings, sir," he said. "Take what time you need."

Daniel entered the church, and his footsteps echoed in the empty nave. A single figure knelt in prayer near the altar, it was his mother, her head bowed beneath a black veil.

"Mother," he called softly.

Elizabeth Bailey turned, rising quickly at the sight of him. She rushed down the aisle and embraced him, her thin frame trembling.

"Daniel," she whispered. "My brave, foolish boy."

"I'm sorry," he said, holding her tightly. "I never meant to put you in this position."

She pulled back, studying his face. "I've never been prouder of you," she said fiercely. "Never doubt that."

"How bad is it?" Daniel asked.

"Worse than I anticipated." Elizabeth guided him to a pew. "He's formally disowned you. The legal documents were drawn up yesterday removing you from the family. Your name is forbidden in the house."

Daniel took a deep breath, "And you? Has he forbidden you from seeing me?"

A small, defiant smile touched her lips. "He may try, but there are some matters in which even Edward Bailey cannot command absolute obedience."

"I don't want to make your life any harder," Daniel said.

"My life has been hard in ways you cannot imagine," Elizabeth replied. "But seeing you stand up for what's right has given me more joy than you know."

"Did you get the bank book? It's not a fortune by Bailey standards, but enough to start a new life."

"I can't take this," Daniel protested.

"You can and you will." Elizabeth closed his fingers around the book. "I've waited twenty years to use this money for something worthwhile. Helping my son begin an honest life seems fitting."

"What will happen to you?" Daniel asked the question that had been haunting him since London.

"I will continue as I have," Elizabeth said simply. "Your father needs me more than he'll admit, especially now that the industry faces scrutiny."

"He'll punish you for helping me."

"He'll try," Elizabeth agreed. "But I've endured worse."

She reached up to touch his cheek. "Promise me you won't disappear completely. Write to me through Lord Ashworth. Let me know you're well."

"I promise." Daniel covered her hand with his. "And if things become unbearable with Father…"

"I'll find you," she assured him. "But my place is here for now. There are still girls who need help."

Tears stung Daniel's eyes. "I never understood until recently. How much you've done, how much you've sacrificed."

"We each fight our battles in different ways," Elizabeth said. "You chose the public stand I never could make. Your testimony might truly change things for mills across England, not just your father's."

"The committee seemed unmoved," Daniel admitted.

"Committees often are," Elizabeth acknowledged. "But the newspapers aren't. The Northern Review's coverage has been picked up by London papers. People are talking, Daniel. Questions are being asked that can't be easily dismissed."

They sat in silence for a moment, mother and son in an empty church, saying a goodbye neither wanted to acknowledge.

"I should go," Daniel said finally. "Arthur's waiting with the carriage."

"Arthur?" Elizabeth looked surprised. "He's with you?"

"Father dismissed him."

A smile touched Elizabeth's lips. "Good. You'll need someone you can trust."

She embraced him one final time, holding him tightly as if memorizing the feel of her son in her arms. "Go with my blessing," she whispered. "Live a life worthy of your conscience."

Daniel held her close, knowing this might be the last time he saw her. "I love you, Mother."

"And I you," she replied. "Now go, before they discover you're here."

Daniel walked back through the nave, and he turned for one last look. Elizabeth Bailey stood straight and dignified, her face wet with tears but her expression resolute. She raised her hand in farewell.

Outside, Arthur sat waiting on the carriage, his posture as correct as always. Daniel climbed up beside him rather than taking the passenger seat.

"Sir?" Arthur raised an eyebrow at this breach of protocol.

"I think we're past 'sir' now, Arthur," Daniel said wearily. "I'm no longer the heir to anything."

"Old habits," Arthur replied, a ghost of a smile touching his lips. "Where shall we go?"

Daniel stared down the road stretching before them. The question encompassed more than just their immediate destination, it was his entire future, suddenly unwritten and unknown.

"I don't know," he admitted.

## CHAPTER 26

*Sarah - Three years later*

Sarah pushed a loose strand of hair behind her ear and surveyed her small shop with satisfaction. Bolts of fabric lined the shelves in a rainbow of colors, and a half-finished dress hung on the mannequin by the window. Bits of thread and fabric scraps littered the floor beneath the cutting table, evidence of a busy day.

"Lucy, make sure you sweep before you go," Sarah called to her assistant, a bright-eyed girl of sixteen with nimble fingers and a quick mind.

Lucy looked up from the bodice she was stitching. "Yes, Miss Dobbs. Will you be back before closing?"

"No, I need to fetch some buttons and thread from the market." Sarah untied her work apron and hung it on a peg by the door. "Lock up when you're done, and I'll see you tomorrow."

She grabbed her shawl and basket, pausing at the small mirror to check her appearance. Three years in Manchester had been good to her. Her face had filled out, her dark hair was neatly twisted into a bun, though rebellious strands escaped no matter how many pins she used.

"Mrs. Winters says we're to have dinner at her place tonight," Lucy reminded her. "She's making her famous lamb stew."

Sarah smiled. "I haven't forgotten. Tell her I'll bring fresh bread from Barrett's if I'm late."

The bell above the door jingled as Sarah stepped onto the bustling Manchester street. Two years, and she still marveled at the difference between this life and her old one. No more cotton dust filling her lungs, no more endless hours standing at machines, and no more cruel overseers monitoring her every move.

"Afternoon, Miss Dobbs!" Mr. Peterson called

from his bookshop across the way. "Fine day, isn't it?"

"Lovely," Sarah agreed, waving to the friendly bookseller.

The market square buzzed with activity, vendors calling out their wares while shoppers haggled over prices. Sarah threaded her way through the crowd toward Hilliard's Notions, her favorite stall for sewing supplies.

"The usual, Miss Dobbs?" Mrs. Hilliard asked as Sarah approached.

"Black and navy thread today, and those mother-of-pearl buttons if you still have them." Sarah set her basket on the counter. "Mrs. Blackwell's dress is nearly finished, and she's particular about the buttons matching exactly."

Mrs. Hilliard chuckled. "Aren't they all? Let me see what I have."

Sarah waited, mentally reviewing her list of orders. Mrs. Blackwell's dress needed finishing, and then she could start on the Milford girls' school uniforms. Business was steady, not enough to make her wealthy, but sufficient to afford a small room above the shop and food on the table. After years of mere survival, it felt like abundance.

"Here we are." Mrs. Hilliard placed a packet of buttons in Sarah's basket. "Anything else today?"

"That's all, thank you." Sarah paid and turned to leave, bumping directly into a tall man who'd been examining fabric at the next stall.

"I'm so sorry," she began, looking up. The words died in her throat.

Daniel Bailey stared back at her, his eyes widening in shock.

"Sarah?" His voice was barely audible above the market noise. "Is it really you?"

Sarah clutched her basket tight. He looked different, his face was leaner, and his clothing simpler but well-made. The polished young gentleman had been replaced by someone more weathered, more substantial.

"Daniel," she managed. "I... this is unexpected."

He laughed, a short, disbelieving sound. "That's putting it mildly. I thought you were still in Lancashire."

"No, I... we moved to Manchester. Almost three years ago now." Sarah glanced around, suddenly conscious of standing in the middle of the busy market. "What about you? I thought you were in London."

"I was. For a while." Daniel ran a hand through

his hair, a gesture so familiar it made Sarah's chest ache. "I've been in Manchester for about two years, actually."

"Two year?" Sarah echoed. "But how…"

A vendor shouted behind them, nearly knocking them over with a cart of potatoes.

Daniel touched her elbow lightly. "Could we… would you have time for tea? There's a café just around the corner. I'd love to hear how you've been."

Every instinct told Sarah to refuse, to walk away before old wounds reopened. But curiosity and something deeper won out.

"Alright," she said. "Just for a few minutes."

The café was small but clean, with checkered tablecloths and windows that let in the sunlight. They sat at a corner table until the waitress brought their tea.

"So," Daniel said finally. "Manchester."

Sarah nodded. "Mrs. Winters sold her bakery in Lancashire and bought a new one here. She invited Annie, Tommy, and me to come with her."

"That was generous of her."

"She's a generous person." Sarah stirred her tea, watching the liquid swirl. "Annie works at the bakery with her. She and Tommy got married last summer."

Daniel smiled. "I'm glad to hear it. He always seemed smitten with her."

"He was. Still is." Sarah took a sip of tea, using the moment to collect herself. "What about you? Why Manchester?"

"After the parliamentary hearings, going back to Lancashire wasn't really an option," Daniel said. "My father made sure of that."

"I heard about the hearings. Your testimony made quite an impact."

"Not enough," Daniel grimaced. "The committee's recommendations were weak. They promised to do more inspections and forced the mills to improve their safety. But at least it started a conversation."

"Bailey's Mill was shut down," Sarah said. "Did you know that?"

Daniel looked up, surprise evident on his face. "No, I hadn't heard."

"Six months ago. The Northern Review ran a big story about it. Your father refused to implement the new safety measures, and when there was another accident—a bad one—the authorities finally stepped in."

"What happened to the workers?"

"Most found positions at other mills. Some, like Tommy, had already moved away. The ones who stayed said conditions improved after the hearings, even before the closure. The fine system was abolished, at least."

Daniel sat back, absorbing this information. "I hoped things would change, but I never expected my father to lose the mill entirely."

"He didn't lose everything," Sarah explained. "From what I hear, he still owns several smaller factories. But Bailey's Mill itself is closed."

"And my mother? Have you heard anything about her?"

Sarah shook her head. "No, I'm sorry."

Daniel nodded, disappointment evident in his face. "We exchange letters occasionally, through my mother's cousin. She's still with my father, though I gather it's not an easy situation."

"I'm sorry," Sarah said again, meaning it.

"Enough about the past," Daniel said, forcing brightness into his tone. "Tell me about you. What are you doing in Manchester?"

Sarah's face lit up despite herself. "I have a little shop. Dressmaking and alterations, mostly. Nothing fancy, but it's mine."

"That's wonderful," Daniel said, his smile genuine. "You always had skilled hands."

"Mrs. Winters helped me set it up. I've even taken

on an assistant." Sarah couldn't keep the pride from her voice. "What about you? What brings you to the market today?"

"School supplies, actually." Daniel pulled a crumpled list from his pocket. "Chalk, paper, slate pencils. I run a small school on the east side of town."

Sarah blinked in surprise. "A school?"

"For working children," Daniel explained. "Evening classes, mainly. Reading, writing, basic mathematics. Children who work during the day still deserve an education."

"That's—that's wonderful," Sarah said, genuinely impressed. "How did you start it?"

"With my mother's money, initially. And Arthur's help—he came with me after we left Lancashire. Now we have three other teachers, and about sixty students."

"Arthur stayed with you all this time?"

Daniel smiled. "He claims he had nothing better to do, but I think he enjoys teaching more than he ever enjoyed being a valet."

Sarah took another sip of tea, studying him over the rim of her cup. "You seem happy."

"I am, mostly," Daniel admitted. "It's not the life I was raised to expect, but it's one I can be proud of."

They fell silent, the weight of unspoken words hanging between them.

"Annie's expecting a baby," Sarah said suddenly, changing the subject. "In about three months."

"That's wonderful news," Daniel replied. "And Tommy?"

"Terrified and thrilled in equal measure," Sarah laughed. "He works as a mechanic now, fixing factory machines. Turns out all those years of breaking them taught him exactly how they work."

"And Mrs. Winters?"

"Flourishing. Her new bakery is twice the size of the old one, and she's got three girls working for her now." Sarah glanced at the clock on the wall. "Oh! I didn't realize the time. I should go—I promised to help with dinner."

"Of course." Daniel stood as she gathered her things. "Would you—that is, could I walk you back? It's on my way."

Sarah hesitated, then nodded. "Alright."

Outside, the afternoon had mellowed, golden light slanting between buildings as they walked side by side. Neither spoke for several minutes, both acutely aware of the other's presence.

"I looked for you," Daniel said finally. "When I first came to Manchester. I asked at all the textile factories, thinking you might have found work as a knotter again."

Sarah's step faltered slightly. "You did?"

"Yes. I wanted to know you were alright." Daniel kept his eyes on the street ahead. "After everything that happened."

"Why?" The question came out more sharply than Sarah intended.

Daniel stopped walking, turning to face her. "Because I never stopped thinking about you, Sarah. Not once in two years."

Sarah clutched her basket tighter. "Daniel, don't."

"I'm not asking for anything," he said quickly. "I just—seeing you today was unexpected, and I couldn't let you walk away without telling you that."

A cart rumbled past, momentarily drowning out all other sounds. Sarah used the interruption to gather her thoughts.

"I'm glad your school is doing well," she said when it was quiet again. "The children are lucky to have you as a teacher."

"Sarah—"

"It's getting late," she interrupted. "I need to go."

They resumed walking, the awkwardness between them thicker than before. When they reached the corner where they needed to part ways, Sarah stopped.

"My shop is just down there," she said, gesturing.

Daniel nodded. "The school's in the opposite direction, near the factory district."

Another silence fell, both unwilling to say goodbye yet unsure how to continue.

"Do you remember," Daniel said suddenly, "what you said to me in the library, that last day in Lancashire?"

Sarah looked up at him. "I said many things that day."

"You said, 'Maybe in another life. One where you weren't born a Bailey and I wasn't born an orphan.'" Daniel's eyes held hers steadily. "I've thought about those words a lot."

Sarah's breath caught. "Daniel..."

"I'm not a Bailey anymore," he said softly. "Not in any way that matters. My father disowned me, legally and otherwise. And you—you're not defined by being an orphan now. You're Sarah Dobbs, shopkeeper and dressmaker."

"What are you saying?"

"I'm saying maybe this is that other life." Daniel took a small step closer. "Maybe this is our chance to see if those differences that seemed so insurmountable two years ago still matter now."

Sarah felt dizzy, her heart racing. "It's not that simple."

"Why not?" Daniel's voice was gentle. "We're different people now. The world around us is different."

"Because..." Sarah struggled to articulate the fear that gripped her. "Because I built this life from nothing, and it's safe, and it's mine. What you're suggesting... it's a risk I don't know if I can take."

Daniel nodded slowly, understanding in his eyes. "I'm not asking for an answer today. Or even tomorrow. Just... think about it? Maybe we could start with dinner sometime."

Despite everything, Sarah felt a smile tugging at her lips. "Dinner?"

"Or lunch. Or tea. Or a walk in the park on Sunday." Daniel smiled back, tentative but hopeful. "Whatever you're comfortable with."

The rational part of Sarah's mind screamed caution, but another part—the part that had never quite forgotten the conversations in that dusty library—whispered of possibilities.

"Sunday," she said before she could change her mind. "The park near the town hall. Three o'clock."

Daniel's eyes lit up. "I'll be there."

"This doesn't mean—"

"I know," he assured her quickly. "Just two old acquaintances catching up. Nothing more unless you want it to be."

Sarah nodded, clutching her basket like a shield. "I should go."

"Until Sunday, then." Daniel tipped his hat slightly, a gesture both formal and endearingly awkward.

As Sarah walked away, she felt his eyes following her. She didn't look back, though part of her wanted to. Her mind raced with questions, doubts, and a spark of something that felt suspiciously like hope.

Maybe this was their other life after all. Maybe some barriers could be crossed, given enough time and change. Maybe.

She allowed herself a small smile as she turned the corner toward her shop. Sunday would tell.

"What happened afterward?" Sarah asked. "With Bailey's Mill, I mean."

Daniel set down his cup. "It was shut down, actually. Six months ago. My father refused to implement the new safety regulations, and after another serious accident, the authorities finally stepped in."

Sarah's eyes widened. "I had no idea."

"He still owns several smaller factories," Daniel continued. "But Bailey's Mill itself is closed. It's rather ironic because all those years of fighting against even the smallest reforms ended up costing him everything he was trying to protect."

"And the workers? What happened to them?"

"Most found positions at other mills, from what I hear. Conditions have improved across Lancashire since the hearings and the fine system was abolished, at least." Daniel's expression softened. "I like to think the small rebellion made some difference."

"It did," Sarah said with certainty. "How is your mother? Is she well?" Sarah asked carefully.

Daniel's face tightened slightly. "We exchange letters occasionally, through my mother's cousin. She's still with my father, though I gather it's not an easy situation."

"I'm sorry," Sarah said, meaning it.

"Enough about the past," Daniel said. "Tell me about you. What are you doing in Manchester?"

Sarah's face lit up. "I have a little shop. I make dresses and do alterations, mostly. Nothing fancy, but it's mine."

"That's wonderful," Daniel said, his smile genuine. "You always had skilled hands."

"Mrs. Winters helped me set it up. I've even taken

on an assistant." Sarah couldn't keep the pride from her voice. "What about you? What brings you to the market today?"

"School supplies, actually." Daniel pulled a crumpled list from his pocket. "Chalk, paper, slate pencils. I run a small school on the east side of town."

Sarah blinked in surprise. "A school?"

"For working children," Daniel explained. "Evening classes, mainly. They learn reading, writing, and basic mathematics. Children who work during the day still deserve an education."

"That's… that's wonderful," Sarah said, genuinely impressed. "How did you start it?"

"With my mother's money, initially and with Arthur's help. He came with me after we left Lancashire. Now we have three other teachers, and about one hundred students."

"Arthur stayed with you all this time?"

Daniel smiled. "He claims he had nothing better to do, but I think he enjoys teaching more than he ever enjoyed being a valet."

Sarah took another sip of tea, studying him over the rim of her cup. "You seem happy."

"I am, mostly," Daniel admitted. "It's not the life I was raised to expect, but it's one I can be proud of."

They fell silent for a while.

"Annie's expecting a baby," Sarah said suddenly, changing the subject. "In about three months."

"That's wonderful news," Daniel replied. "And Tommy?"

"He's terrified and thrilled in equal measure," Sarah laughed. "He works as a mechanic now, fixing factory machines. Turns out all those years of breaking them taught him exactly how they work."

"And Mrs. Winters?"

"She's flourishing. Her new bakery is twice the size of the old one, and she's got three girls working for her now." Sarah glanced at the clock on the wall. "Oh! I didn't realize the time. I should go... I promised to help with dinner."

"Of course." Daniel stood as she gathered her things. "Would you... that is, could I walk you back? It's on my way."

Sarah hesitated, then nodded. "Alright."

Outside, the afternoon had mellowed, and golden light had started slanting between buildings as they walked side by side. Neither of them spoke for several minutes, both acutely aware of the other's presence.

"I looked for you," Daniel said finally. "But I didn't know where to start from."

Sarah's step faltered slightly. "You did?"

"Yes. I wanted to know you were alright." Daniel kept his eyes on the street ahead.

"Why?"

Daniel stopped walking, turning to face her. "Because I never stopped thinking about you, Sarah. Not once in these three years."

Sarah clutched her basket tighter. "Daniel, don't."

"I'm not asking for anything," he said quickly. "I just… seeing you today was unexpected, and I couldn't let you walk away without telling you that."

A cart rumbled past, momentarily drowning out all other sounds. Sarah used the interruption to gather her thoughts.

"I'm glad your school is doing well," she said when it was quiet again. "The children are lucky to have you as a teacher."

"Sarah…"

"It's getting late," she interrupted.

They resumed walking, the awkwardness between them thicker than before. When they reached the corner where they needed to part ways, Sarah stopped.

"My shop is just down there," she said, gesturing.

Daniel nodded. "The school's in the opposite direction, near the factory district."

Another silence fell, they were both unwilling to

say goodbye yet unsure how to continue.

"Do you remember," Daniel said suddenly, "what you said to me in the library, that last day in Lancashire?"

Sarah looked up at him. "I said many things that day."

"You said, 'Maybe in another life. One where you weren't born a Bailey and I wasn't born an orphan.'" Daniel's eyes held hers steadily. "I've thought about those words a lot."

Sarah's breath caught. "Daniel..."

"I'm not a Bailey anymore," he said softly. "Not in any way that matters. My father disowned me, legally and otherwise. And you... you're not defined by being an orphan now. You're Sarah Dobbs, and you're a shopkeeper and dressmaker."

"What are you saying?"

"I'm saying maybe this is that other life." Daniel took a small step closer. "Maybe this is our chance to see if those differences that seemed so insurmountable two years ago still matter now."

Sarah felt dizzy, her heart racing. "It's not that simple."

"Why not?" Daniel's voice was gentle. "We're different people now. The world around us is different."

"Because..." Sarah struggled to articulate the fear that gripped her. "Because I built this life from nothing, and it's safe, and it's mine. What you're suggesting... is a risk I don't know if I can take."

Daniel nodded slowly. "I'm not asking for an answer today. Or even tomorrow. Just... think about it? Maybe we could start with dinner sometime."

Sarah smiled. "Dinner?"

"Or lunch. Or tea. Or a walk in the park on Sunday." Daniel smiled back. "Whatever you're comfortable with."

"Sunday," she said before she could change her mind. "The park near the town hall. Three o'clock."

Daniel's eyes lit up. "I'll be there."

Sarah nodded. "I should go."

"Until Sunday, then." Daniel tipped his hat slightly, a gesture both formal and endearingly awkward.

As Sarah walked away, she felt his eyes following her. She didn't look back, though part of her wanted to.

Maybe this was their other life after all. Maybe some barriers could be crossed, given enough time and change. Maybe.

She allowed herself a small smile as she turned the corner toward her shop. Sunday would tell.

ALSO BY SYBIL COOK

The Cobbler's Daughter

A moving tale of hardship, love, and resilience in the heart of Victorian England.

1874, Lancashire—With her father's cobbler shop failing and his health fading fast, **Annie Sutherland has no choice but to take on the burden of keeping a roof over their heads.** But times are changing, and fine handcrafted boots are losing out to cheap factory-made goods. **With customers dwindling and the landlord's threats growing louder, Annie's world is closing in.**

Then there's **Tom Hartley**, a mill worker with troubles of his own. **A man who knows what it is to struggle, to go without, to fight for every penny.** When fate throws them together, Tom sees Annie's pride and stubbornness for what they truly are—desperation. And though she doesn't want his help, he can't stand by and watch her lose everything. But help comes with a price, and when **ruthless moneylender Silas Drake offers Annie an escape at a cost she dares not name, she is faced with an impossible choice.** Take the devil's bargain, or risk everything to hold on to the only life she's ever known.

A tale of love found in the darkest of times, of dignity and defiance in the face of ruin. Perfect for fans of Catherine Cookson and Dilly Court, Sybil Cook's latest saga will have you turning the pages late into the night.

DOWNLOAD NOW

Printed in Great Britain
by Amazon